AN EMORY CRAWFORD MYSTERY NOVEL

THE DEVIL'S FLOOD

by Pearl R. Meaker

PROMONTORY
PRESS

Promontory Press
www.promontorypress.com

ISBN: 978-1-987857-57-3

Cover Design and Typeset by Edge of Water Designs, edgeofwater.com

Printed in Canada
987654321

"The Good Lord willin'
and
the creek don't rise."

Traditional American Expression

"People think that at the end of it all
we become just a pile of bones
in a six foot hole.
But the truth is—what we really become—
is a story."

Megan Macedo

PROLOGUE

IT SEEMED THE YEAR OF 1844 WOULD SEE NAUGHT BUT RAIN AND MORE rain, though in fact there had been days of sun and relative dryness. On one portentous day, coming down from the monochromatic slate sky, there was not a bit of it being a light rain that fell. Not one bit. When it wasn't pourin' buckets full that obscured one's vision as effectively as a blizzard, it was like a fine sheer curtain hanging over the window of the world, filtering the view into soft, wet, edgeless shapes painted in drab watercolors.

The road heading west out of Twombly had been flooded out several times in many spots and Sandy Ford across Okaw Creek and Slippery Ford across Rock Creek were under water as often as they were above. Folks on both sides of Okaw Creek kept riding out to the ford, just northeast of the oft-flooded fields where Melvin Sutton farmed—sharecropped to be exact—to see if the way was passable for a single rider or a team and wagon. Most often it wasn't.

On that day, they didn't even bother.

On that evening they stayed home.

On that night a large part of the physical world they'd known would be changed.

CHAPTER 1

CRUNCH!

"Mmm." I sighed.

Crunch! Crunch, crunch!

"Oh. Yeah!" I whispered.

"Darlin', are you eatin' that salad or having an intimate relationship with it?" Jebbin asked me, his Ozark accent stronger than usual, warm and sweet as hot cocoa.

My eyes popped wide open as I chewed and swallowed as fast as I could. Not an easy task when eating a hearty lettuce salad.

"Ah, what do you mean?" I mumbled around my last few chews.

"'Mmm!' 'Oh. Yeah!'" He mimicked. "I know when I usually hear my darlin' Emory goin' on like that." His blue eyes twinkled behind his glasses.

I swallowed. "I was not doing that."

My dear hubby nodded. "Oh yes you were. Just like Bill Murray's character in *What About Bob?*"

Grinning, I shook my head. "That bad, huh?"

"Yep. Every bit as."

Usually it's Jebbin who makes the yummy sounds while eating and me who brings up *What About Bob?*

"Well, it isn't my fault. I have no idea why it is but my homemade chef's salads never taste as good as the ones we get from Gulatto's. They are an ecstatic experience meant to be savored." I thought for a moment. "Maybe it's the pepperoni? I never have it around the house so I don't have it in the ones I make."

We shared a companionable laugh over our lunch. We were outside, under one of those large white plastic canopy things that people use at weddings or for booths at outdoor arts and crafts fairs. Three sides had matching white plastic walls to keep out the rain that was blowing from the west; the fourth side was open to the south and offered a view of the grey, choppy surface of the currently flooded Sutton's Lake. It had been yet another in the seemingly endless series of rainy days that were threatening to make this a record year for flooding in central Illinois.

Jebbin and I weren't alone in the pavilion. There were eleven other people. We usually ate all together or split into two groups, one of students and one of non-students. But, whether it was because of the weather or something else, today people were either sitting by themselves or coupled. We were all part of an actual *bona fide* archeological dig in Golden County, just a few miles west of Twombly.

"I will try to contain myself," I said before plunging another forkful of delight into my mouth and crunching happily away.

Jebbin finished his own bite of salad. "You're right. Gulatto's chef's salad is better than yours. Sorry, Hon."

I nodded my agreement, trying hard not to make any more contented noises while savoring every crisp succulent chew.

An early morning fiasco at our house had resulted in our having the carryout from Gulatto's. Our Golden Retriever, Sophie, had an accident on the living room carpet and Hortense, one of our two cats, urped up in our bed—fortunately after we were out of it for the morning—resulting in us not having time to pack our lunches, the way we usually did. Jebbin had volunteered to do a lunch run into town before we rushed out the door, then asked our fellow digging crew members if anyone else wanted something from Twombly's best Italian restaurant before he left the dig site. Most everyone had packed a lunch, but a few did have Jebbin get them a side salad or some tiramisu for dessert.

There hadn't been a dig in Golden County since around twenty years ago when a mammoth tusk had been found near Okaw Creek, and nearly fifty people had applied to be on this new project under Dr. Chauncey Koerner, (C.K. or "Ceek" to his close friends), a history and archeology professor at Twombly College.

Nineteen of us made the final crew to begin with, but when it became clear that the winter's snow and spring rains were hanging around to become a summer monsoon season, our numbers rapidly dwindled to ten, not counting Ceek. We had Jebbin and me. Jebbin because—well, I wasn't sure why he'd put our names on the list, other than that, like me, he'd been moody lately. It made sense to me, I wasn't used to dealing with crime and murder like he was, being the head of the Golden County Forensics Lab, and two cases in less than a year that I ended up deeply involved in was not my norm. But my good man was just … off. He had me worried. I think doing the dig instead of just hitting a lot of bluegrass festivals over the summer was helping. And yet …

Me? I think I made the crew as a kindness to Jebbin after he mentioned a few times to certain people that we had *always* wanted to do a vacation together on a dig. That was an exaggeration. I knew about it because a couple of them brought it up to me, which I think he hadn't anticipated. We had said a few times over the years that a dig might be fun but had never made any serious attempt to follow up on the idea. So, a lie on his part, again *not* normal for Jebbin, but I was glad I'd been given the opportunity and we got to spend a lot of time together.

Our youngest non-student was Nancy Walker, a late-thirty-something adjunct professor in the art department who taught photography and the fine art of Photoshop. Nancy was the official photographer for the project. She had experience as well—she really *had* taken vacations as part of dig crews. Oscar Hornsby, a retired ophthalmologist and personal friend of Ceek, was the oldest person on the crew. The four of us made up the non-student members. Well, technically, we had five older adult non-students, but Dr. Koerner is our leader, not part of the crew.

With the college footing a lot of the bill, it had been required that a majority of the crew be students. After the exodus in the first week, they were only a majority by one. We had Kate Epperson—an environmental anthropology major. She hoped we'd find the family's garbage pit. Dan Martin and Hank Cervellone—archeological anthropology majors—hoped we'd find the house somehow intact, so they could study the style of its construction and date any materials and tools found. Mack Black, a sociology major, and Ronnie McLaren, a history major (our other female student) were both interested in the stories that had arisen about the house and its inhabitants over the past hundred and seventy years or so.

And there was one more team member, Melva Suter. At first she had orbited around the edges of the group and that had been fine with most of us, as she didn't fit in well. Her lack of response to friendly overtures had put people off. Added to that she was younger than everyone else, being between her junior and senior years of high school, and was working the dig for course credit to help raise her GPA. She was a problem kid and the principal, who was another friend of Dr. Koerner's, got her a place on the dig since the only courses she seemed to put much energy into were history classes. Her unkempt hair was dyed a faded fire-engine red. The T-shirts hanging on her too thin frame slapped you with various vulgar sayings. When she wore jeans they had holes that showed her underwear and when she wore shorts her tush peeked out below their frayed edges.

The only thing that didn't fit her rebel image was the hat she wore, as all of us were required to, on sunny days. It was a cute, natural color, raffia bucket hat with what I was sure were two handmade peach colored crocheted flowers with orange button centers secured to the left side. It was the hat that opened her up to me a little. When I told her how cute it was on her, a gentle smile graced her drawn face. A soft glow filled her usually dull eyes.

"Really? You like it? You think I look good in it?"

My "compliment smile" grew more genuine. "Yes to all. You look adorable. Where did you get it and do you know if someone made the flowers that are on it?"

Melva's smile faded but the glow in her eyes grew happier. "It was my mom's and she made the flowers. I had a kid's size hat like it and she made the flowers for each hat, you know, so we matched." She paused and looked away across the lake. "She died when I was ten. I outgrew my hat so I took the flower off and put it on hers 'cause hers fits me now." She added a "thanks for liking it" over her shoulder as she turned and walked away. It was one of the few times I'd heard her talk without cussing nearly every other word.

Melva set off something with my "knowin's", the intuition I inherited from both of my southern grannies, that attracted me to her, despite the fact that most everything about her seemed to push me away like matching poles on magnets. So many things about her demeanor, vocabulary, and body language put me off. But since the day I had complimented her hat, she often worked or sat near Jebbin and me, occasionally exchanging brief comments with us. And she would sometimes bring something for our lunch from her dad's restaurant, The Coal Bin. Not to share, mind you, but handed to us before she'd move a little ways off to sit alone despite our invitations to join us.

And that's where she was today as we were eating our lunch—about six feet or so away.

"Do you think we'll find the house?" Jebbin said softly, hoping, I reckoned, that none of the others would hear.

It wasn't an encouraging question.

"No." The mood and volume of my words matched his. "But then, as I've told you, it doesn't help that we don't know exactly where the house was to begin with."

I had done more research about the whole situation than Jebbin had. He'd had his fall and spring classes to teach and various other responsibilities. And me? Before and after the situation we'd had in January, with the murder of Jairus Twombly's personal assistant and a kidnapped student, I hadn't had anything else that needed my attention. Researching the story of the Sutton House had been my form of therapy after January's murder while Jebbin relied on me to fill him in whenever he had questions about it.

"The old maps we have don't distinguish the farm from the rest of the land in the area. They just have 'Mr. Sutton farms here or something like that written in the general vicinity. We haven't found a plat map for the area so there's no property lines or details of who owns what parcels of land. And, as usual, accounts of the incident differ. Some say the house was on the north side of the road from Twombly, others on the south side. They couldn't even agree if it was the road from town that crossed at Sandy Ford or the one that crossed at Slippery Ford."

"Umm," he mumbled, nodding. "Usual result of rumors. Like the ones going round Twombly this summer about some powerful new drug or drink being used at teenage parties." He shook his head, looking displeased. "Lots of talk and nothing solid to check on, like everything else."

"That's an understatement." I agreed.

There had been five editorials in the paper about the stuff rumored to be available at the parties, three of them saying it wasn't as bad as rumor claimed and the other two saying that it was going to be addictive or kill a lot of kids. I heard conversations about it everywhere in town. I set my last bite of salad aside. The mention of the parties had killed my appetite.

"I know the Sutton House disappearing riled things up the same way. Newspapers throughout Golden County said it was everything from a wandering magician to God's angels swooping down to claim it. Or that a local witch lady cursed it, or that everyone in the county should be in a panic because Satan himself had sucked it all down to Hades and might take their home next."

We both sat in silence for a few moments, mulling over the gossip of rural people in 1844.

"I suppose nowadays folks would say it was aliens." Jebbin chuckled and winked at me, trying to lighten our moods. "Who else could make a house disappear off the face of the earth, or out of flood waters as is more likely the case, overnight with no wreckage left behind?"

"People are f'ing mean."

The low-voiced words were spat out like something vile tasting. We both looked over at Melva.

She glared back at us for a moment then edged across the few feet between us.

"I'm a Sutton," she continued in a voice I was sure wasn't carrying to the others in the pavilion. "It was my great-great-great grandfather who disappeared that night and my great-great-great grandmother who was widowed. Our family all know she had to f'ing go back to using her maiden name so her kids wouldn't get teased and bullied at school after it all happened. That's the only reason I've shown up here every day is to find out if he's here somewhere so that maybe he can get a decent burial or something and finally shut all the stupid, mean, f'ing people around here up."

Jebbin and I stared open-mouthed at her. We weren't used to that much bad language. Melva stood up but didn't move to leave. I'd never seen her look so strong—or so fierce—even though tears ran down her face.

"Some of us need those f'ing parties. And if you guys tell anybody who I am, you'll regret it."

Melva Suter-Sutton turned sharply then strode stiffly out into the rain.

The rain had stopped but the air was still heavy with moisture as I sat on a sheet of plastic tarp gently working my way around something that might have been a piece of pottery. You really never knew until you worked it free, and I let my mind mull over what Melva had said and Ceek's reason for this dig being done.

What could make a house vanish overnight?

The question kept swishing around in my head like the wind and rain on the pavilion earlier. Because we weren't just looking for a foundation …

We were looking for the entire house.

And, for perhaps the first time, I was wondering if we were looking for a body as well. Melva's great-great-great grandfather. A picture of her proud, angry, tear-wet face popped into my mind.

Let's face it, even if the flooded convergence of Okaw Creek and Rock Creek had washed the house away in the Great Flood of 1844, there should have been pieces of it caught up in the trees that, according to all the accounts, were still standing along the course of the two waterways. There had been plenty of remains of the farm's outbuildings, but one thing every account agreed on was that not one scrap of debris from the house was ever found.

And no bodies.

It wasn't until mail got through to Twombly from Xanthe, a small town in north Golden County, that it was discovered that at least Polly Sutton and their eight children hadn't disappeared with the house. Three days before the mysterious event, Melvin had sent them to be with some of her family who farmed to the west of Xanthe on land that hadn't flooded.

Polly's brother-in-law wrote to say that they were all fine, but Melvin had stayed behind at the house.

No one ever found out what happened to Melvin Sutton. Like the house that had been provided to the Sutton family by the man he sharecropped for, Melvin had disappeared. What remained was a legend and a lake bearing his name … and a very angry young descendent.

"What was that?"

The cry brought me out of my reverie to see Ronnie McLaren leap to her feet.

A second later we all felt a tremor.

Jumping up, we all clumped together as if that would help against … whatever was happening.

"Look!" Nancy pointed toward the shoreline a few yards away from the pavilion. She then started clicking away at it with her Canon.

The water's edge twitched.

I'd never seen water twitch like that. It did it again …

… And then it started to slide away from the shore. With an explosive roar and a huge plume of spray, the water ripped through the levee a hundred or more yards due south of where we stood.

Within moments the water's edge was ten feet lower and twenty feet further away.

CHAPTER 2

"MY GOD!" DR. KOERNER EXHALED. "IT'S A GOOD THING WE'RE OVER here. I'd given some thought to checking around on the levee side of the lake, in case the road and the ford had actually been over there at one time."

The levee kept Sutton's Lake separate from the quarry where a sand and gravel company had found a good-sized deposit of gravel under a fallow field Melvin Sutton had once sharecropped. They hadn't wanted the water from the lake to interfere with their quarrying, even though quarrying always brought up water on its own and had created ponds and lakes wherever they dug, so they had built the levee.

There was a collective intake of breath, an exhale, then everyone was talking.

"What do we do now?"

"Do we call the college?"

"Or the cops?"

"Yes, should we call 911?"

"Do you think Sutton's Lake will keep draining into Rock Lake?"

I looked over to my left.

Jairus Twombly suddenly appeared around the eastern corner of the pavilion and everyone hushed. It's just something he does. He knows when things are amiss. He usually knows where and sometimes even what has happened. I have a touch of intuition, too, and had had the feeling that someone was approaching the pavilion.

After nodding to the group, he turned to look at the water. "That should make looking for the house easier—if it is here to find." Jairus turned back to address our bedraggled bunch. "Anyone hurt?"

No one answered. I shook my head and reckoned that's what everyone else was doing.

"Good, no need to call for emergency services. Actually," he glanced back at the shrunken lake, "no need to call anyone." Looking at us and with a twinkle in his eye and a grin he added, "Not like we can pour it all back in."

The tension broke as everyone laughed.

"I know it's early to call it a day," Ceek said to Jairus, "but can we call it quits? We've had enough excitement and the rain water is starting to work its way under the pavilion walls, so it's getting soggy where we're working."

"Of course." Jairus smiled and nodded. "It's supposed to be sunny tomorrow and drier. The same on Thursday. I suggest you take tomorrow off, let the surface dry out a little, and come back on Thursday. Use the day to think of what newly exposed areas you want to check out first, C.K."

"You heard the boss, everybody." Ceek put on his professor's voice. "A day off tomorrow. Relax. Goof off. Rest up and be here six a.m. on Thursday, all clean and shiny and ready to get dirty."

We headed for our cars parked along the edge of the road. I noticed that those ahead of me kept glancing back. Jebbin and I did too, still needing to see the lowered level of Sutton's Lake, needing to be sure the burst levee had really happened.

"Emory? Dr. Crawford?"

We stopped walking. We hadn't noticed Melva come up on the side of us away from how we'd turned to see the lake.

"Can I … um … get a ride to The Coal Bin from you guys? Dad won't be coming for me until three or so. You know, between the lunch and dinner crowds. I, uh, hate to call him to come early. There's a lot of prep work that gets done around then." She looked ill and what little color she'd had in her face had drained away like the lake behind us.

My mom instincts kicked in. She was obviously over her earlier outburst and letting us into her life again.

"Of course, Melva. Glad to help out."

"Thanks." She didn't move toward the cars, only turned to look back and forth at the wide expanse of newly exposed lakebed. She shivered and hugged herself. "It's like … like, oh my God, could this really happen now? We could really find the house and … and …" Another shiver shook her. "And who knows what else."

Jebbin gently took hold of her left arm and I moved to her right side. We walked slowly through sand and mud that were still heavy from the day's rain and humidity.

"Yeah, we just might." Jebbin's accent was more pronounced, his tone as comforting as chicken soup when you have a cold. "We jus' might. And we'll keep yer secret, just like ya asked us to. We'll be right here with ya and we'll help ya through whatever happens."

I was glad there was always an afghan in our back seat. Mostly there for times when Sophie came for a ride, but always changed out for a clean one if she'd used it, so it was always fresh. I tucked Melva up and we headed into town.

"It's gonna be too weird if we find it." Melva sounded more like she was talking to herself than to us. "I mean, just … yeah. Weird.

I was excited before. Ya know? But now that the water's moved out of the way … Who'da thought the water would move? Even that's creepy. Now I'm not so sure I want us to find the house. Maybe it'll just be creepy, too."

She was quiet for a moment or two.

"Thanks for the afghan, Emory. I … I musta got cold. I'm warmer now. Thanks."

"You're welcome, Melva. Glad it's helping."

We arrived at The Coal Bin and took her in. Her dad, Larry Suter, thanked us for bringing her home and, noticing that she wasn't looking well, told her to go lie down on the couch in his office. I was happy he did. She looked beat. We told him what had happened at the dig, that Dr. Koerner had given everyone tomorrow off, said our goodbyes and headed home.

"Dinner out tonight, Mrs. Crawford?" Jebbin queried as he pulled out of the restaurant's parking lot.

"Sounds great, Dr. Crawford—after a hot shower. Cracker Barrel? I'd say The Coal Bin but I think Melva could do without a reminder of what happened today when she's trying to work tonight."

"Excellent choice. Dinner at Cracker Barrel with cuddling on the couch watching *The Murdoch Mysteries* afterwards?" He draped his arm across my shoulders.

"Mmm … yeah. That sounds wonderful," I cooed, and leaned into his shoulder.

⌒

Wednesday morning found me taking Sophie for a walk on the Twombly campus. Twombly's campus excelled at beautiful, with several large open areas that were used for everything from student sunbathing (bathing suits mandatory) and pick-up sports to sites for various fairs and other open-air community events. Then, there were the various gardens. We had the Fountain Garden—where, unfortunately, Dr. Archibald Finlay Dawson was murdered, the Japanese Garden—where, also unfortunately, Dr. Timothy Law was murdered, and the J.M. Ramm Music and Science Garden—where thankfully no one had been murdered.

Today, Sophie and I headed for the new Furever Friends Garden. It's the largest garden on campus with all sorts of things that make it fun for people and their pets. It's circular and enclosed, excepting where the arched entry way cuts through, with a ten-foot-wide dog run with ten-foot-tall fences to keep even the most agile dogs inside. The wide run gives dogs lots of room to romp, with specially constructed obstacles for them to run through and over. The gate to the run is in the outside fence next to the gate to a separate area, complete with free doggie-doo bags and trash cans, where you can take your dog before letting them into the run. Inside the ring formed by the dog run is the garden proper with trees, plants, picnic tables, and benches. In one area there are eight individual cat enclosures with platforms and tempting hanging toys for the kitties to bat at. Another area has smaller enclosures for small pets like rabbits and ferrets. There is even a section with enclosures for reptiles. The whole garden is kept meticulously clean by pre-veterinary students and Twombly townsfolk who love animals.

Our kitties, Hortense and Kumquat, stayed home, preferring the comforts of our screened porch. But Sophie adored the garden, and I brought her often.

I took Sophie to the "business" area, cleaned up, then unclipped her leash and let her go into the dog run, closing and latching the gate behind her.

When I turned to look around, I was surprised to see Madison Twombly over by the cat enclosures.

I hadn't seen much of Madison since summer break started. She was taking a community education jewelry making class in the morning three days a week, mandolin lessons at the music shop one afternoon a week, and she and her mom together were doing summer stock with The Twombly Troubadours who put on two musicals each summer. Right now they were rehearsing *The King and I.*

"Madison!" I called over to her.

She looked up from the book she was reading. "Emory! Come here, I have the most wonderful thing to show you."

I plopped myself down and gave her shoulders a hug. "I've missed you. How are you, and how's your mom?" Amy Twombly had been the primary suspect in a murder last January. She was completely exonerated, but it had left its mark on her. Mostly good marks. She was trying to think less about herself, less about being a rich man's wife, and more about how important her husband, children, and friends were. She had long been a rather snooty pain in the rear and often still was, but she was doing better with that, too.

"Mama's doing really well, mostly." The young teen gave me a wink. "It's got to be hard to change how you've behaved when you've done it most of your life. But she's doing her best. "How about you? I heard about the levee bursting and was really glad it was nowhere near the dig."

"I'm fine. Jebbin's fine, too. We're looking forward to having a day off today. Dr. Koerner suggested it and your Dad agreed that it'd be good to let the ground dry a little today and go back at it tomorrow."

She nodded. "Hmm. Yeah. A day off and drier ground sounds like a good idea to me. I have time tomorrow late morning, and I think I'll pop out there and see what you all get up to."

As Jairus's daughter, Madison could show up and help at the dig and no one would mind, even though she wasn't part of the official crew.

"That'd be great! Come at lunch and I'll make enough ham and pasta salad to share." I got a little more serious. "Do you know Melva Suter?"

"Yes."

I gave her a questioning look. "That's a rather short answer coming from you. Care to elaborate?"

"Well. She isn't someone I hang around with, you know? I mean for starters, she's a couple of years older than me and she's not in, like, band or choir where you get a mix of all the grade levels."

"You're holding back," I prodded.

"She's gone bad. It's not the way she dresses or even the way she talks," Madison quickly amended. "We're all pretty used to that at school, plenty of the kids swear a lot. But she's into bad stuff … or at least that's what I hear from some of the crossover kids."

"Crossover kids?"

"Yeah. They are rough kids that like music enough to be in band or choir, even though most of those sorts of kids think it's all for dorks. So, even though they run with a crowd I'd never run with, I've gotten to know some of them and talk with them. A lot of them are really nice when you get past the cussing and stuff. Makes me wish they weren't into the bad stuff they're into. Anyway, according to them she's one of those 'you name it, she's done it' types."

Madison looked over at the cat enclosures. I could tell there was more to come so I didn't push her.

"Her mom died and I can't imagine going through that. Then after that … she had to quit some of the things she was into, like dance and swimming. I think it was just hard for her dad to figure out how to take her around to everything when he needed to be working at their restaurant. I don't think he made her quit to be mean or anything. He and her mom had started The Coal Bin just a few years before she died and I've heard my Papa say they did a lot of the work themselves. So I don't think they had many employees to cover things."

My young friend looked over at me and sadly shook her head.

"Family can be so hard sometimes," she said before looking away again. "I've got the feeling she started feeling trapped. Kinda normal teen stuff but worse because of the situation. You know, loves her dad, wants to help, wants to be a kid too, but she's old enough that she's probably thinking she's ready to be on her own. It had to be a huge jolt to lose her mom and the activities she loved. I've heard she was a really good dancer and swimmer, and had even won some competitions."

In the space that followed Madison's revelations about Melva, I decided that I'd have to get over the uncomfortable vibes the surface me got from the girl and pay more attention to my intuition that was telling me she needed someone like me. She had been reaching out to Jebbin and me, and now I was thinking we needed to make a better effort to reach out to her. My back tingled and I smiled with the knowin' that it was the right thing to do.

"Now, you said you had something to show me?"

"Mama finally let me have a kitten."

Amy didn't care for pets. Too messy. Too smelly. Too furry or too scaly (which was worse). Just plain too much bother.

"Oh, my! Really?" I looked at the cat enclosures. "Which one?"

Madison pointed. "He's in the second one from the right."

In the cage was an adorable white kitten with a pale orange striped tail and legs, and peachy ears with a frosting of peach on his back. His face showed a hint of an orange striped mask and big blue eyes.

"He's a flame point Siamese," she said proudly. "That's a mix of an orange tabby and regular Siamese. He's only about fifteen weeks old and his orange color points will get darker as he gets older but the background color will stay white."

Her kitten was happily batting at one of the hanging toys.

"He's adorable, Madison. How long have you had him? Did you get him from a breeder?"

"I've had him over a month. We got him from the New Start No-Kill Shelter." She reached over and placed her left hand on my forearm. It was a gesture more common to older people, but Madison is an enigma.

"Someone found him by a road when he was seven or eight weeks old. He couldn't have been there long, a mostly white kitten would be easy prey, but it was long enough to get the respiratory and gunky eye problems that abandoned kitties get. And he was all scraped up too. He either got tossed from a car or blown around when vehicles went by."

"It seems strange that someone would dump a part Siamese cat."

"Well," Madison looked over at him with a loving smile. "He's a special needs kitty. He's a little wobbly, and he's deaf. That's probably why he was dumped. But he's a happy little guy."

I hugged her again. "I'm glad you have him, Madison. What have you named him?"

She laughed. "That's the best part. Last spring, I went to science day at school. You know, Twombly College science students come and do cool demos hoping to get students interested in science. Like who isn't interested in science? Well, one of the demos was dropping a Cheetos snack into a test-tube with some heated potassium chlorate and, wow! This really huge flame shot out the open end of the test tube. I'm sure you've seen it, Emory. They called it the Flaming Cheeto. I thought of naming him that because he's a flame point and his tail looks like a Cheeto."

She pulled out her iPad and typed something on it without letting me see.

"You've got to see how it's spelled." She handed over the tablet.

Flaming Chi To

"The 'Chi To' part is to make his name look Asian, you know, since he's part Siamese."

"That's so cool, Madison. I'll have to tell Jebbin. He'll love it."

"I thought of him when I came up with it." Her smile faltered a bit. "I've got some other news, not as good."

"What?" I said in my caring "mom" voice.

"You know I'm doing the plays with the Troubadours?"

"Yeah."

"I'm doing crew, which means I'm basically invisible. Not what Mama wanted, but that's another matter. Because most everyone ignores crew people, I … ah … get to eavesdrop."

No surprise there. Madison and I are both incurably curious.

"And?"

She looked down, avoiding looking at me. "Plays are another place where you get a big mix of different people. Among the non-adult cast and crew there's all this talk about some new booze at weekend parties. You know what I mean?"

"Yes, I know. There've always been weekend teen parties." I sighed. "Melva said something to us the day the levee broke. She didn't say it outright, but I think she goes to the parties. With what you've heard about her being a 'you name it, she's done it' type I got one of my feelin's that she's involved with the illegal gambling that's rumored to be going on in the county as well. I know they have gambling machines at The Coal Bin and I bet she can get into the restaurant when it's closed. That might be awfully tempting."

Madison shrugged. "If it's really going on, I wouldn't put it past her, sad to say. The booze at the parties, whatever it is, they're saying it's really strong and some kids are getting out of control. There've been some bad fights … people getting pretty banged up. The kids I overheard …" She looked up at me. "They act like it's funny but I get the feeling it's going way too far."

I nodded. "You're telling me this, why?"

Madison picked up a soft-sided cat carrier, went to the enclosure, took Flaming Chi To out, and zipped him into it.

She looked over her shoulder at me. "I'm going to be checking it out."

That's all she said before running, cat and all, from the garden.

I didn't try to follow her. Couldn't have caught her if I'd tried. I texted her later in the day to ask if she was still going to come out to the dig on Thursday for lunch, which we broke for around 10 or 10:30 a.m. since we started at 6:00 every morning. I reminded her that I was making a batch of my ham and pasta salad, which I knew she loved. She said she'd be there. And I knew I could wait till then to find out more of what she meant by "checking it out".

Madison arrived earlier than lunchtime Thursday morning, curious to see the effect of the levee break, and to be part of the crew's activities for the day.

The newly exposed ground was surprisingly dry. Wednesday had been unusually hot and dry all day with a stiff westerly wind, and this morning had been the same. Everyone was wearing hats today, even the students, on Ceek's orders, and we all carried water bottles. Dr. Koerner had made it clear he didn't want to deal with any sunstroke on this dig. We could all scuff down a few inches with our boot toes before the sandy-dirt-crusty muck of the former lakebed showed signs of moisture. Even then, it was barely damp for another inch or two before it became thick but still not soggy with water. A test dig had found the soggy layer was only around six inches thick, then faded back to packed clay. This had been the base of the lakebed. Ceek said it was likely that much of the mucky part of the lake bottom had been lost when the water rushed out because it should have been a few feet thick.

We had invited Melva to join our search group so it was Jebbin, Melva, and Madison and I walking along, abreast in a line and spaced about five feet apart. The two girls seemed to have hit it off and I was glad to see it—even if part of it was apt to be Madison "checking into" the parties. Madison, like her father, had a way of getting along with most everyone. We were kicking and scuffing at the ground, pausing to dig or poke with our "probes"—slightly sharpened three-foot-long pieces of old rebar—if something caught our eye. As far as we knew, no one had found much other than shells, buried former driftwood, glass bottles, and beverage cans.

I noticed the girls had gone quiet and I took advantage of the break to ask Madison my burning question.

"What did you mean by you're going to be checking out the parties?" I quietly asked Madison as we walked along.

"For now, I'll mostly keep listening to their stupid boasting about how drunk they got and all the," she made air quotes, "*fun* things they do … And which guy or girl they did them with."

I nodded. "Yeah, that's always been part of it, too. Thinking it's so cool, until it isn't."

"Yes. Yes, that's it. I mean, there's quite a few of us, the teens in the play or ones on the crew, who want nothing to do with it, but the ones who go just try to make us feel like losers."

"Yep." I sighed and shook my head. "That hasn't changed either."

I looked over past Madison and Melva and saw that Jebbin was no longer in line with us. I stopped and looked around. The girls followed suit.

Jebbin was about twenty feet behind us, poking the ground around him with his rebar. The bar was sinking in about a foot before stopping.

"Find something, Dr. C.?" Melva called.

"I don't know." His puzzlement showed in the questioning tone in his voice as he stared at the bar he kept poking into the earth. "I seem to be hitting something but can't tell if it's solid or hollow or …"

With a crunch, a splintering crash, and a stifled cry, my husband vanished from sight.

CHAPTER 3

FOR A MOMENT NOTHING MOVED …

Or made a sound …

"Jebbin!" I screamed. I tried to run up the slight slope to where he'd been, but seemed to slog through the sandy soil like a wobbly toddler.

"Emory, stop now!" Dr. Koerner yelled.

I ignored him but Madison caught up to me despite the sand, grabbed me, and pulled me to a halt. Melva stumbled up on my other side.

"Oh my God, Dr. Crawford!"

I heard her shocked exclamation, though it sounded like it came from far away.

"Jebbin!" My own voice rang shrill in my ears.

Harsh.

Desperate.

"Jebbin!"

I batted at Madison's hands, jerking my arm to get away.

I froze as his voice floated up from the ground. "I'm okay, Honey. Okay." Fainter than a scream. Stronger than normal talking.

I wasn't all that convinced by his words. "Jebbin! Are you hurt?"

"I'll be okay." His voice was already less strong than before. "You help 'em out up there."

I didn't want to help out up there. I wanted to go down that hole and be with my dear man.

Arms engulfed me, squished me in a hug.

"He's okay! He's okay." Melva bounced me up and down. "I would've been so pissed off if he'd been killed or something. He'll be okay. Grandpa Melvin will watch over him. I always figured that his ghost or something was still stuck in the house and he won't let anything horrible happen to the guy who's set him free. He'll be okay. I know he will," she babbled on. "You'll see, Emory, Madison. It all just got buried. No evil magic or curses. We aren't a cursed family! It's gonna be okay."

Her monologue ran on but, even though I was returning her hug in kind, my mind had shifted back to what my honey had called up to me from out of that hole: "*You help 'em out up there.*" Whether I liked it or not, Jebbin was right. I'd be in the way down there. I jumped when I heard a shout.

"Kate!" Ceek barked the order.

"Yes, Dr. Koerner."

"You rock climb, don't you?"

I looked over at the petite, slender girl. She looked as if the prairie wind that was blowing could send her rolling along the newly exposed beach. She did rock climbing? But then again, I suppose it helped not having much of your own weight to lift.

"Yes, sir."

"Mack, you're closest to the road. There's rope in the back of my truck."

"Got it!" Mack raced off.

"Jebbin!" I hollered again. I needed the reassurance of an answer, no matter how faint it might be.

"Here. Still here. Haven't gone anywhere."

Had anyone called 911? Was anyone doing anything? I started forward. Melva's hug and Madison's grip both tightened.

"No, Emory." Madison had a tone like her daddy, a natural authority not easy to ignore.

"No, Emory." Melva's input entreated instead of commanded.

"Yeah." I settled back on my heels. "Yeah. I'll stay put."

"Kate," Ceek addressed the girl again. "You're the lightest one on the crew. You'll need to belly-crawl to the hole, just like you're going across ice to get someone who's broken through. When Mack gets here … oh! You're here. Mack, help her tie that around herself however she wants it. She'll know what she needs. We don't know where the edge of …"

He turned toward where Jebbin's voice was coming from. "Jebbin? Are you in the house?"

We all hushed. We hadn't even … well, *I* hadn't and I now had the feeling none of us had even thought about what sort of hole he had fallen into. Except for Melva and Ceek. She had loosened her hold on me and I was able to look at her face. It showed an incredible mix of emotions; the joy that had had her bouncing us, relief that my husband—and her new friend—wasn't grievously injured as far as we could tell, and fear. She was blanched with fear. I felt like I could hear her mind shouting, "Is the house really what's down there, or am I hoping too much?"

"If it isn't the one … we're looking for, then … there's two houses buried … out here," came the now strained voice down the hole.

We all started cheering.

Even me.

For five seconds. Maybe less.

Then our brains reminded us that there was someone stuck down inside a buried house and the cheers faded feebly away.

Kate quickly tied a kerchief over her mouth so it looked like a surgical mask and dropped to the unpleasant looking ground. Let's not forget—until two days ago it *had* been the bottom of a lake. A regular lake with fish, water birds, and all sorts of other things … eliminating in it. I wouldn't have wanted to breathe close to it either.

She was moving rapidly in a very weird manner. Like a crab or a hovercraft skittering and floating over the ground. I looked closer.

She was clearly a rock climber indeed!

Kate moved gracefully toward the hole, her flat front an inch or so off the ground, up on her fingertips and toes. We knew she'd arrived when she lowered herself.

"Hi, Dr. Crawford," she said down the hole. Turning to look over her shoulder she asked, "What do you want me to do now, Dr. Koerner?"

"There's a chopper!" Dan Martin pointed eastward toward the sky over Twombly where the dragonfly machine could barely be seen racing our way. Jairus Twombly's Mercedes pulled up at the roadside as though towing the helicopter that was coming up fast behind him.

I could see him scanning our group.

"Jebbin's the one in trouble then, Ceek?" he asked as he walked up to Ceek, his shiny dress shoes and the bottoms of his expensive trousers now dull grey with lake bottom dust. Jairus' intuition hadn't let him know the "who" of the situation this time. Like me with my lesser gift, we never knew what information our insight would give us.

Jairus called over to Kate. "Ask Dr. Crawford if he's hurt, where, and to hazard a guess how badly."

We couldn't hear her talking to Jebbin, the chopper was up high and about a mile south, but was still making enough noise to garble it, and she was talking down into the hole. Eventually, she looked back at us.

"Yes, he's hurt and shaken up. Both legs and left arm. Right leg worse." She broke off to smile. "His right foot or leg might be broken, but since he doesn't want it to be he won't say it is. Left leg was maybe just jarred a bit too hard. He put his left arm back to break his fall backwards when he landed and hopes the fall is all it succeeded in breaking. Just a sec," she added, turning back to talk to Jebbin, then back to Dr. Koerner. "He says the rescue guys will need to make a couple more trips down there, and you should call Dr. Conti at the hospital pathology lab. He says he's got company down there."

"Company?" Several of us said it in near perfect unison.

I felt Melva tremble. Her face went from pale to white with a grayish tinge around her eyes.

"Grandpa Melvin?" she whispered from her colorless lips.

"Chopper One?" I heard Jairus say into a walkie-talkie before he turned and stepped away from the group.

Kate pulled a ball of twine from a side pocket of her cargo pants. She tied the end around a belt loop, unwound several lengths of it and threw the ball toward us. "Someone get that and tie on a jacket or something I can lay over the edge of the hole." Nancy had a lightweight jacket tied around her waist and soon it went scooting over to Kate as she reeled it in. She arranged it where she wanted it, turned, and lowered her legs into the hole then hollered. "Keep a good hold on my harness rope as you pay it out; then keep it taut but not tight. Be ready to gradually haul me up when I give it two tugs." She slipped over the edge.

Within a couple of minutes Hank and Mack were pulling her up, and she worked her way back out. She did her crab walk back just as the first rescue worker began his descent from the chopper. Madison had moved from hanging on to my left arm to Melva's right side. I had hold of Melva's left hand, Madison had hold of her right, and we each had our free arms wrapped around her waist.

"Okay." Kate said, pulling her phone out of a pocket as Jairus and the crew gathered around me where I stood watching the rescue team go in after my husband. "Here's a shot of Dr. Crawford." She held the phone in front of me. "He's still conscious and managed a little wave, but I'm glad the rescue team is heading in."

I glanced at the photo. Jebbin lay in a pool of light on what looked like a pile of bedding heaped on a rough wooden floor. His glasses had fallen off. He never looks quite right without them, and I could tell he was hurting. Probably feeling a bit nauseous as well. In spite of it all he wore a wan grin and had lifted a hand in greeting.

Kate swiped the screen.

In the sharp glare of her phone's flash a mummified man sat on the floor, his back against a wall. There was a dark stain spilling down his chest from a hole near where his heart would be.

"There's one part of the company Dr. Crawford mentioned."

She swiped again. "Here's the other."

This mummy lay on its back. The flash showed a stain that flowed from his chest and down his side to form a hardened puddle on the floor.

"Which one's my Grandpa?" Melva gasped.

Everyone's gaze moved from the photo on Kate's phone to the shocked teenager Madison and I were holding onto.

She jerked a hand free to clap it over her mouth. Her eyes were wide in horror. "I shouldn't have said that," came muffled from behind her hand.

I shot a pleading look to Jairus Twombly.

With the team gathered close to look at the photos, there was no need for Jairus to speak loudly.

"Ladies and gentlemen." All eyes turned to him. "You are all officially instructed that you are not to repeat anything that has been said."

The Twombly Touch had its usual effect. Everyone nodded in unison.

But Melva spoke up. "No. Really. Ah … um, thank you, Mr. Twombly. I, ah. It's been a secret all this time but now that the house …"

With a limp hand she gestured toward where the house lay open to the world for the first time in one hundred seventy years.

"Everyone's gonna know it got found. Don't see how that can be kept quiet. And everyone will start wondering about the family again and news people will start looking into it and … I think it will all get figured out anyway. Polly Sutton went back to her maiden name of Suter. Changed her kids' names as well. The family didn't stay long at her sister and brother-in-law's farm near Xanthe. She moved 'em all up to Normal, started her sewing business, and it was like no one made the connection to Melvin Sutton and the House That Vanished."

She looked around at everyone. The faces I saw looking back at her wore expressions of wonder, as though Melva Suter had risen up out of the mysterious old house, a flesh and blood incarnation of a legend.

"I … I guess I just would like to tell my dad about it first. So if it'd be okay, could you guys not say anything to anyone until you know he knows?" She frowned suddenly and looked uncomfortable. "Well maybe till I say it's okay. I don't know how he'll take it or what he's gonna want to do about it." She looked at Jairus. "Is that okay, Mr. Twombly?"

He smiled his wonderfully reassuring smile. "That'll be just fine, Melva."

Madison and I hugged Melva and we joined everyone else and watched as supplies went down into the house after the paramedics. It seemed an interminable amount of time before a rescuer on a second rope came down to help guide the rescue basket through the hole they had enlarged in the roof. As his head cleared the opening, Jebbin looked around till he spotted me and gave me a thumbs-up before he was lifted over our heads and into the chopper.

Melva squeezed my hand. "I'm really sorry Dr. Crawford got hurt finding Grandpa Melvin's house, Emory. I sure do hope he'll be okay."

I mustered more confidence than I felt. "I'm sure he's not hurt too badly, Hon. No one's fault," I reassured her.

But I had the feeling Jebbin was hurt worse that it seemed.

The second helicopter that had arrived and landed nearby took to the air to deliver two forensic team members and two more rescue workers to the opening into the house by cable.

Jairus touched my arm. "Let's get you to the hospital, Emory, and get Melva home to her dad. You too, Madison," he added, and we all walked toward their Mercedes. "I'll have an officer take your car home, Emory. I think you're better off not driving right now." He answered my concerns before I'd even expressed them. As usual.

I stopped walking. "Can Madison stay here?" I asked. "I … ah, I think Melva and I both want a good full report of everything that happens out here. Jeb …" My voice caught on his name. "Jebbin will, ah, want it, too, when he's … ready for it." I realized my hands were shaking.

"On it!" Madison grinned then scampered back to the crew before her father could say otherwise.

"Marple and Drew," Jairus muttered, smiling as he shook his head.

"Yep." It was all I could think to say as he opened the front passenger door of the car for me before opening the rear door for Melva. My mind was completely focused on getting to Jebbin.

CHAPTER 4

I TRIED TO REMIND MYSELF THAT HOSPITALS ARE PLACES PEOPLE GO TO get better.

Yes.

They aren't just odd smelling places where scary procedures happen.

But …

I was scared, it smelled like a hospital, and I had no idea how hurt my husband really was.

Jairus came back to the hospital after taking Melva to The Coal Bin and kindly offered to stay with me in the waiting room.

"How are you holding up?" he asked as he sat in a chair next to me in the waiting room.

"I'm not sure. I guess okay. How was Melva doing by the time you dropped her off?"

"I had her move into the front seat, mostly so I could have a look at her. She was still looking pretty shaken up. I went into the restaurant with her; I wanted to make sure her dad was there. He wasn't too happy to see her home early and all upset again. He asked what trouble she'd gotten into now, seeing as she was being sent home before the usual time."

Jairus reached over and took hold of both my hands. As soon as we touched, a strong tingling ran up my back. I knew Melva hadn't been able to tell the news about the discovery to her father the way she'd wanted to.

"You and Melva had to tell her dad about the house and all right away, didn't you?"

He nodded. "Yes. I think she was scared because of his reaction to her coming back early, since his first thought was she was in trouble again. Larry sounded angry, but the look on his face was closer to despair. I was picking up such confused emotions from him. He swore and asked her what she was thinking, and what were they going to do if she wasn't allowed back."

I could see it and hear it in my mind.

"She walked out on him, didn't she?"

Jairus nodded with a wry grin on his face. "Your intuitions are getting stronger all the time, Emory. Yep. That's exactly what she did, though 'stormed out' would be more accurate, and not before she ran him up one side and down the other."

I grinned. "I'm sure she did. Let's see … 'why do you always think I did something bad, you don't even give me a chance,' ending with 'she's out of there' and 'don't expect her back for her shift at work.' Did I get it right?"

Jairus chuckled but followed it with an exasperated sigh. "Yes. She sounded like any teenager would, except with her history I'm sure both her dad and I were more concerned than some parents would be." He breathed in, closed his eyes, and shook his head. "All my gift is getting on her is a generalized bad feeling. I've no idea what she's going to do." He took another breath. "That said, Larry asked me what the hell had happened so I figured I'd better tell him."

"Even that we might have found his ancestor? That there were mummified bodies in the house?"

"Yep. I told him all of it. Told him we'd found the house, that Jebbin had fallen through the roof of it, and that there were two mummified male bodies inside. Then I told him Melva, in her shock, had slipped and muttered something about one of them maybe being her grandfather and that I'd ordered the dig team to keep that in confidence until he'd been told and we knew what he wanted to do about it.

"And?" I encouraged.

"It took the wind out of his sails. He even pulled a chair out from a nearby table and sat down. Asked me to repeat it all. Hollered to one of the staff to pull him a draft beer and chugged half of it, then sat there for quite a while repeating *who'da thought* and *oh my God.* Finally, he thanked me for bringing Melva back into town. He apologized several times for jumping on her case, which I told him she needed to hear, not me. In the end he thanked me for telling the crew to keep quiet about it and that he'd send word with Melva tomorrow about what they wanted us to do—adding that if he didn't see her before then, he'd give Dr. Koerner a call to let him know."

I shook my head. "Not something I'd want to deal with," I said, and then a thought came to me. "But who knows? It might be great for business at The Coal Bin. I know the restaurant does well but this could really draw in a crowd."

We talked on about other things, like wondering how Jebbin was doing and what might happen next at the dig, for about an hour when Amy Twombly showed up. She hugged me tight and expressed genuine concern for Jebbin. When she finished the hug, she handed me a bamboo crochet hook, a ball of lovely blue-green acrylic yarn and a pattern for a washcloth, so I'd have something to do with my hands while I waited. Then she sternly told Jairus it was time he came home and they both left. She was improving in her attitudes and level of human kindness, but she was still Amy.

I chuckled about it and started crocheting. I would've rather had the needlepoint I was currently working on, but at least it was something to do. The needlepoint was of Katsushika Hokusai's famous woodblock print "The Great Wave off Kanagawa". I had started it before the announcement that there would be an archeological dig to find the legendary house that disappeared in a flood. Since then, my "gettin' a knowin'" feeling would sometimes slither down my back as I worked on the picture of a mighty wave inundating part of Japan with Mt. Fuji in the background. Odd that I had chosen that classic piece of art to stitch.

I was only eleven rows into the washcloth when …

"Sticks and string as usual, I see."

I grinned, dropped the crocheting onto the chair next to me, stood, and hugged my best friend and my boss at the Twombly library where I volunteered, AnnaMay Langstock.

"Stick singular," I said, "and sticks and strings are nicer than sticks and stones." I gave her a squeeze. "Thanks for coming."

"Where else would I be once I could escape my library?"

We hugged a moment longer then sat down.

"What time is it?"

"Have you eaten?"

We chuckled at our simultaneous questions.

She looked at her watch. "Twelve-thirty," she replied to my question.

I'd been here about two hours. "No, I haven't eaten," I replied.

"I'll be right back." AnnaMay went to the nurses' station and returned holding up a dark, flat, plastic thing. "A pager like at restaurants. They'll buzz us when there's word about Jebbin. Let's get you something to eat. You're looking peckish."

It's fun having someone around who occasionally uses good

old-fashioned words, and I was suddenly feeling peckish. I stuffed the crochet things into a pocket of my pants since I'd left my 'dig bag' with my wallet, keychain, and other such items in our yellow Beetle, which was now, I presumed, at my house since Jairus said he'd take care of it.

We headed off but I pulled to a stop just a ways down the hall to the cafeteria.

"I can't go in there." I waved my hands at my clothes. "I'm filthy. These are my dig clothes."

She looked me up and down. "No. You're not too bad," she said, swatting at my butt and swiping at my knees. "Really, not bad at all. This is a hospital. People come in here from all sorts of situations. I'm sure no one will think a thing of it." She gave a couple of pats to a patch of dust on my left thigh. "You're good. Come on."

"Yes, ma'am." I saluted my friend, the former Air National Guard staff sergeant.

"Got that right, airman."

We laughed as we marched to lunch.

We were nearly done with our ham and cheese sandwiches, chips, and conversation about the bodies Jebbin had found in the house, when the pager went off.

"You scoot." AnnaMay waved me off. "I'll clean up here then head over to the library to start gathering up materials for you to look through."

Her sharp look froze me in place.

"I'm not mistaken in thinking that you're going to stick your nose into this business of The Mummified Bodies in the House at Sutton's Lake, am I? You'll need info on mummies themselves and, as memory serves—and mine serves me well—you haven't asked to access anything from the Golden County Historical Archives yet. I would offer you access; actually, I'll do that anyway. That way if you do need to get away from the dig and a possibly grumpy Jebbin, you can go into the archives room. But I'm thinking, since Jebbin is hurt and things will be picking up a great deal at the dig, you're going to be terribly busy now and won't have much time to spend in the library. I'll scan everything I can find that I feel will be pertinent and put it all on a flash drive for you."

I grinned. "No, you're not mistaken and your memory is spot on. Thanks for getting all that for me, you're a dear! I know I'm going to need it. I feel it in my gut that there is going to be more to this than just finding the house. And I know the mummies, whoever they may be, are just the beginning."

Receiving her nod of acknowledgement, I turned and race-walked out of the cafeteria.

⁀⁾

"Surgery and the pain meds have him knocked out for now, Mrs. Crawford, and he'll most likely sleep until late tonight or tomorrow morning. Don't get worried if he sleeps that long."

Dr. Christopoulos, the orthopedic surgeon, stood across from me, on the other side of Jebbin's bed. I was mostly staring at this man with the answers but kept darting looks at Jebbin. I know it sounds silly to say but he looked so tired, even though he was asleep.

The doctor looked at the iPad in his hand. "We'll start at the bottom and work our way up. Your husband fell approximately eight feet through a hole in a roof. His injuries indicate that he landed right foot slightly ahead of his left on what the paramedics noted as 'an old fashioned rope and straw mattress bed', and the ropes appear to have given only slight resistance before they broke. I'm quite sure that his injuries would have been much worse if that hadn't slowed him down a little and provided some cushioning. Still, he has a traumatic fracture of the calcaneus, or heel bone. We did need to do some surgery on it. It was rather minor, just tidying up a couple of minuscule bone fragments. He'll be in a walking cast." Dr.

Christopoulos looked up at me. "That's actually a bit of a misnomer, at least at first. He is to be non-weight-bearing for a while."

He looked back down to read.

"He also has some sprained, that is stretched, ligaments in his right ankle. Oddly, he only has mild sprains in his knee. It will just be achy for a few days or so."

Another look my way.

"Are you doing okay, Mrs. Crawford? Is this making sense to you?"

"I ... ah." I looked around for a chair.

The doctor said, "Here," and moved the only one in the room next to me, and I sat down.

"Um, yes. Yes, it's making sense. Please go on."

"He appears to have mostly surface bruising to his left leg. Maybe some mild sprains to his ankle and knee, but nothing that a wrap support or elastic bandage can't handle. We scanned his lower back." He looked at me again. "Usually there is damage to the lower back, even fractured vertebra in that region, in feet-first falls, but Dr. Crawford seems to have fallen loosely instead of tensing up. That, and perhaps the bed and mattress, seem to have helped him avoid more serious injuries to his legs and back. He might want some light back support for a while. Eventually, he'll be getting physical therapy just to make sure everything gets built back up as it should. Next ..."

"Next?" I was beginning to wonder how I was going to manage taking care of Jebbin when he came home. He's six feet tall and around one hundred ninety pounds. I'm five foot five and ... pudgier than I should be. If nothing else, I don't have the height to have good leverage, lifting or supporting someone his size.

Dr. Christopoulos looked at me again. "You weren't aware he'd hurt his arm? I, ah, yes. I have a note here that he had mentioned it to someone at the scene."

I remembered. "Oh, yes. He said he'd put his, ah ... left hand back to break his fall."

"Yes. That's my 'next'. He has serious sprains in his wrist, ah, that's stretched ligaments with a few micro tears. It should all heal up without surgery, but for now his wrist and forearm are in a removable cast. He also has badly sprained ligaments in the elbow and shoulder but no tearing in those joints. He'll be in the cast for a while and he'll need to use a sling for a couple of weeks, maybe more. How long he has to use the sling depends on how quickly the sprains in his elbow and shoulder heal."

He paused, but neither of us said anything so he continued.

"He probably would have injured his head as well, but again, the mattress offered some cushioning. He might have a stiff neck for a day or two, but otherwise his head is okay."

Another pause.

"Your husband will be in a wheelchair for several weeks." He must have noticed my look. "Ah, do you know how crutches work?"

I nodded.

"Even with the forearm design crutch, the hand and wrist take all the weight bearing. We need to be sure his wrist is sufficiently healed before we take him out of the wheelchair and put him on crutches."

"How am I going to take care of him?" My voice sounded hollow in my head.

The doctor came back to my side of the bed and patted my shoulder. "A good honest question, Mrs. Crawford. My answer is don't fret about it. He'll be here all day tomorrow, possibly longer if he has any complications or seems to need the higher level of care for another day or two. We have staff who specialize in helping caregivers with just such issues. They'll discuss your home's layout with you before he goes home and help you decide if renting a hospital bed will be of help. They'll also give you numbers for the companies in the area that provide help with in-home care."

"I won't be able to get him in the house." My hollow voice persisted. I felt so helpless. "There are stairs at all three outside doors."

"Hm. Yes, I bet you live in one of the faculty houses. Lovely old homes but that was before accessibility was an issue. Is there a bedroom and large bathroom on the main floor?"

"Yes. All the bedrooms are on the main floor and the master bath is large."

Dr. Christopoulos headed for the door. "That should all be fine, Mrs. Crawford. I'll make a note about needing help getting him into the house, so the home-help staff will have a heads up. I'll see you again tomorrow."

I was alone with my sleeping husband and my thoughts.

CHAPTER 5

THE AFTERNOON TICKED BY.

Nurses came.

Nurses went.

I crocheted. I walked around the hallways a couple of times. I crocheted some more.

I called our kids and left messages. Told them about what happened, about Jebbin's injuries and that their dad was fine. No need to come down and visit, but I was sure he'd like a card and some sort of food gift if they wanted to send him something. I was sure I'd hear back from them sometime this evening.

Jairus called around 5:30. Said he'd talked to Dr. Christopoulos and he'd be talking to the homecare staff and the physical therapist as well in the morning. "I want to make sure Jebbin gets the best available treatments and supplies. We do that for any college staff or faculty member who is hospitalized."

"Dr. Christopoulos said he'd need a wheelchair, Jairus." This was, at the moment, my biggest concern. "How am I going to handle getting Jebbin in and out of a wheelchair? How are we going to get him into the house?"

"I'll make sure it's all worked out, Emory. Okay? Don't worry."

A sigh breathed from my lips. "I'm sorry, Jairus. The doctor told me about the homecare help and all, and now you're assuring me all will be well. I guess I'm just tired and …"

For a long moment there was silence.

"Feeling a little guilty?" he gently asked.

And I wasn't sure what to say because he was right.

"Marple and Drew. Crawford and Twombly. You don't want to be left out."

"That sounds so horrible." My statement should have sounded miffed. I wanted miffed because Jairus was seeing through me. I was too tired for miffed so it sounded resigned.

He chuckled. "No. Not really. I know you and my dear nerdy daughter haven't hung out a shingle or printed up business cards, but I also know you're both irresistibly drawn to mysteries and there's a big one out by Sutton's Lake. You stayed home your whole married life, and …"

I could visualize him holding up a hand to stop the defense that was in my mouth wanting to pop out. Sometimes his 'knowin's' were so annoying.

"… And," he continued, "I know you were happy and content to be there. That you considered that your career. But now you're feeling drawn out of the 24/7 home and family life that is down to just you and Jebbin."

"He's going to need care."

"How many times were you sick and he went to class? Even when he was a student, not just when it was his job. Hmm?"

"Lots. But this …"

"Isn't a job. I know. But it is something you're feeling called to.

Gifted in. I think he'll understand, Emory."

I said nothing.

"Besides, you can be his eyes and ears at the dig. I—well, I've the feeling he signed up for the dig because he was looking for something different. Something that wasn't his usual routine. I think it will help him if you can keep him informed. Let him be the one to do some vicarious living." He hesitated. "And I think he'll be getting some of that 'need for something different' from the challenges he'll have dealing with his injuries; might even turn out to be a good thing."

"You're serious, aren't you?"

Jairus laughed. "Of course. I'll gather up my team of elves and we'll make sure all is well with the good Dr. Crawford and the hospital's merry band of health service providers while you and Madison go investigating." He paused again. When he spoke his tone was serious. "Besides, I don't want Maddy totally unsupervised. If Amy or I nose in, she'll spook and get even more covert than she already is when she's helping you." His voice caught on his emotions. "Or looking into things herself. I know she's doing that, too, and it does worry me. But we know she tells you most of what she's doing and where she's going because you're her partner, as it were. It helps her mama and papa feel better that someone knows what's going on and will let us know if she's stepping out too far. She is rather young despite how mature she often appears to be."

It was my turn to smile. "Yes. I keep all of that in mind when I'm with her. I'll do my best to keep my channels open with her, and you and Amy as well."

"I just now thought of a wonderful solution to part of your problem, Emory. I have some calls to make. I'll get back to you tomorrow morning. Just remember, no need to fret. Get some rest tonight."

And the call went dead.

I went to the cafeteria for dinner. The food there was good and affordable, and I knew a lot of people in Twombly who treated the hospital cafeteria as one more available choice when they wanted an inexpensive meal out.

Back in Jebbin's room, I was watching TV when the phone by his bed rang.

"Hi Emory," Madison replied to my greeting. "How is Dr. Crawford? Are you doing okay?"

"I'm … doing better. Your dad called and I'm feeling better about what's going to happen when I have to take Jebbin home. He fractured his right heel with some sprains and strains in the ankle, knee, and hip on that leg. Though they say the sprains and all aren't as bad as they could have been. Said he must have landed loosely. His left leg is bruised and sprained too, but also not seriously."

"Kate said he fell on a bed, so that must have helped."

"Yep. That's what the doctor said. His wrist isn't broken but badly sprained or strained—wish those words weren't so similar. I get them confused. At any rate, his wrist will be in a removable cast for a while and he won't be able to use crutches because of it. I'm kinda worried about that."

"That makes sense. Yeah. It will be hard for him to get around even in your house in a wheelchair."

We were quiet for a few moments—a comfortable quiet of two friends thinking.

"I bet you'd like to know what happened at the house after you and Papa left."

My voice and lips smiled. "You bet I would. Did you take good notes?"

"Better. It's video and I recorded it."

With a shake of my head and a light huff of a chuckle I said, "Why does that not surprise me."

"Because, you know I am totally the best."

I could picture the lit-up look of pride on her face.

"Do you want to see it? No. Dumb question. You wanna see it. Can I come up? I'm, like, downstairs in the lobby. I wanted to make sure I wouldn't disturb Dr. Crawford or, you know, embarrass him. It's not like I'm your daughter and some people, I know from my volunteering, don't like visits from young people who aren't close family. You know, the whole 'being in bed with a flimsy little hospital gown on' thing."

I looked at my conked out husband. "Come on up, Madison. I don't think it would bother him anyway, but Jebbin's thoroughly asleep from pain meds and just plain being worn out. I'd like the company."

"Be there in a jiffy!" she said and hung up.

A few minutes later a couple of soft taps on the door preceded Madison into Jebbin's hospital room. She brought the earthy smell of a warm, rainy Illinois summer's evening in with her—absorbed into her T-shirt, shorts, and moisture-fluffed blonde hair. A wheeled desk chair was dragging along behind her.

She paused, looked at Jebbin before looking at me, then pulled her chair next to mine.

"It's so weird that they rarely put two chairs in the rooms." For someone who volunteered here, she seemed ill at ease, twisting her hands together before settling them on her bare kneecaps. Her gaze went back to Jebbin. "I'm sorry he got hurt, Emory. The rescue guys who keep buildings, caves, and such from falling on trapped people said it looked as though he'd found the one bad spot in the roof to poke with the rebar. They figured the bar went through first and weakened the rotten spot enough that he went through right after. Someone said it was a miracle Dr. Crawford didn't get impaled on it when he fell."

"Yeah, well." A strong shiver gripped me. "I had thought … while I've been sitting here with him that he could have … but he didn't and I made myself stop thinking about it." A bit of my tension whispered out with an insight I'd just received. "But, oddly, his walking that line and falling through was a good thing." I turned to her as she turned to me with a shocked look. "Not that I ever want him to get hurt," I reassured her. "And I've been thanking the Lord that he didn't fall on that rebar or land harder than he did and be broken up worse than he is. But, we might never have found the house if he hadn't found that one weak spot. What if it had been Kate who had been walking that line? I doubt she'd have been heavy enough to break through. Or if Oscar Hornsby had been there. He's enough older than Jebbin that he could have ended up with some very serious breaks."

"That's a strange way of looking at it, I guess, but I see what you mean."

Madison gave a light shake as though to clear away a sensation she didn't like the feel of. She pulled her phone out of her shorts pocket and her iPad out of the carry case that hung at her left hip.

"Let's watch the video," she said, as she deftly connected the two. "I'll lead into it. Papa left with you and Melva and I had run back to the dig crew.

"At first, the investigators and the rescue team didn't want any of the archeology crew in the house. Dr. Koerner wasn't happy and insisted that a representative of the dig be allowed in. He basically told them it was our dig site as much as it was their crime scene and that Twombly College, who was paying for everything and was represented by his team, needed to be included. About that time, the now Sergeant Henry Schneider shows up. He got called because the house is in Golden County and not within any town's limits." A weary sigh escaped Madison. "I wish they hadn't called him, but I guess I can't always avoid him."

Henry Schneider had been a captain in the Golden County Sheriff's Department when Madison's mother had been accused of murdering her husband's personal assistant with an ornate wooden crochet hook last January. Henry had tenaciously focused on Amy Twombly as his only suspect and came close to interfering with the investigation to push the case against her along. After she was proved innocent via a confession from the real killer, the department felt a disciplinary action was needed. He'd been out of hand on a few other cases as well. For one year he would be a sergeant, to have his former rank restored only if he maintained a high level of professionalism for that year.

"So," Madison continued, "after some debate they all decided that Kate could go in seeing as she'd already been in before the forensic and rescue teams had arrived. They had her suit up like the forensic guys, even though she'd already left trace at the scene—said they figured it'd be best if she didn't bring in any more. In the end it was Kate and two structural engineers, to further assess the house's stability, and two forensic team members. I asked Kate if she had Skype on her phone. She did so I had her call me via Skype so we could see everything." She looked up with her Cheshire Cat grin. "Of course, I knew I could record a Skype video call."

I shook my head and grinned. "Of course you can."

"Well, I'm sure most of the students on the crew could do it too. Okay, on to the recording. I watched it real time, of course, but this will be the first time I've seen it on the bigger screen of my iPad."

A few screen touches later the video began.

CHAPTER 6

"OKAY, I'M BACK IN THE HOUSE." KATE'S VOICE CAME THROUGH CLEARLY.

"The picture is really good." I exclaimed.

Madison paused the recording. "The two tech teams brought in high power lights. They set them up on the surface and arranged them so they shone down into the hole in the roof at various angles so they had a pretty good-sized pool of light down there. Plus they all had head lamps on too." She tapped play.

The video showed everyone staying close to the bed Jebbin had landed on, since that area had already been disturbed, while the two forensic specialists evaluated their crime scene.

"I hadn't noticed much when I was down here before." Kate must have had her phone by her face. It was obvious she was whispering but in the recording we could hear her clearly while the eye of her phone's camera followed the movements of the forensic team. As they worked, Kate kept speaking.

"It's creepier down here than I remembered. I guess I was so focused on Dr. Crawford that I didn't notice much else. I, um, I don't think it's just because this time I know there are mummies here. It just feels ... yeah, well ... creepy. Even though the hole has been in the roof a while now, it still feels cooler in here than outside. And dry, not damp. There's a lot of dust." Kate showed the stuff curling in the air in the bright beams of light. "That's part of the creepiness, I think. It looks like photos of apparitions on the ghost hunter TV shows. I wouldn't have thought there'd be so much, but ... I'm looking around," Kate said, though the camera stayed on the swirling dust, "and I can see there's a thick layer of dust over everything. The walls aren't plumb, and ... ah, the floor isn't level. I don't think I can get a good enough shot of a corner for you to see that things are off square but I can feel it. It's at least a few inches lower on the side toward the lake, that would be, ah ... to the south. Not so bad that everything went sliding all the way to one wall, but it's obvious that things shifted. I'll give you a tour."

The camera moved, slowly, fortunately for me. I can get dizzy if someone pans too fast.

"Here's the bed that Dr. Crawford landed on, that's how we know it's a bedroom. Good lighting here as, duh, it's where the hole in the roof is. When they enlarged it, they extended it toward the foot of the bed and to the side I'm standing on. I'm standing to the west of it, and the headboard is against the south—lake side of the house—wall. It has nightstands on both sides. It's all rather plain furniture. Not rough hewn, but no lathed spindles or intricate carving. Just plain, but well made pieces. There are no oil lamps on the nightstands ... no wait, there's one on each side but they're on the floor. I think they must have fallen when the house got buried. It's strange," Kate paused a moment, "when I bent over to look for them, I could still smell a slight scent of the spilled oil after all this time. That will probably fade now that the room is open to fresh air.

"Okay, I'm turning to my right." Our view changed as she

panned the camera. "You should be able to see a small table with a tipped-over chair partially under it. A large, again plainly built, wardrobe fell forward to land on the table at an angle. It's resting against the small table about three quarters of the way up it. It has a couple of drawers in the bottom part of it that are partially open. A couple of books are on the table; one of them is hanging over the down-slope edge. The table was probably centered under a mirror that's … wait a minute. Let me see if I can zoom in and still have enough light for you to get a good view."

The picture zoomed and we saw what had caught Kate's eye.

"Oh my god! Whoa! That's earth out a window, not a mirror."

There was a slight pause as Kate spoke to the workers around her, drawing their attention to the window.

"We'll have to check this out later, Dr. Koerner," she continued to the archeology team. "A quick look showed us it's the same at a window over a desk on the opposite side of the room. But that's where the mummies are. So, for right now, since we've been told not to move from the bedside until the forensic guys have given us the all clear we can't get a closer look. Guys from both teams looked at it and we all think it's odd that the dirt didn't break through the windows. I'll keep doing my video tour.

"On the same wall as the wardrobe, there's a washstand with the pitcher smashed on the floor beside it. The stand itself is upright. Then we have the door, hanging open like an arrow pointing in the direction of the lower end of the room."

Kate paused again. "And then there's the focus of the forensic team. The, uh, part of the room where the, um, bodies are."

For a few minutes the video followed the crime scene techs without commentary. They had determined where they felt the most crucial areas of the room were, being the two mummies and the area immediately surrounding and between them. They moved to the outer walls of the room, slowly walking the perimeter and around the furniture that was up against the walls. Then, going even slower, they moved inward until each one was next to one of the mummies.

Kate chuckled a little. "This is like watching *C.S.I.* on TV. They're taking photos as they go, and leaving numbered markers by some items, straight or right-angle rulers by others. There doesn't seem to be too much lying around on the floor other than things you'd expect to find in a bedroom. You know," the camera looked from one object to another, "clothes on the floor in a corner. A couple of throw rugs on either side of the bed. Some stuff must have fallen off tables or the desk. Nothing strange except for a small gun on the floor between the two, mum … men. We, ah, can tell they're men because they both have beards, and they're both in shirts and trousers. Women rarely, if ever, wore trousers in the mid 1800s.

"I don't know much about guns, but I'm thinking it is a Derringer of some sort, it's so little. Odd place to find it. You would have thought one or the other of the men would be holding it, or that it'd be on the floor right next to him. But it's almost half way between them; a good three feet from either of them. There's also a small metallic—looks like brass maybe—thing about the same size and shape as the grip of the gun that is on the floor between Man B and the south wall of the room. One of the crime scene guys said he thought it was a powder flask.

"I think the forensic team is going to be doing fiddly stuff with the mummies for a while. Since I can't move around until they say I can, I'm going to save my battery and shut down. If something interesting to our crew happens, I'll start shoot—eh, filming again." The video ended.

Madison backed it up a little and we looked intently again at what Kate was describing. Then Madison paused the recording where we could see both bodies and the gun between them.

"What do you think?"

I leaned closer to the iPad. "Hmm. It doesn't seem … reasonable?

Not sure that's the word I want. Ah. I think Kate's right. One guy having it would make more sense."

"Yep. Just what I thought when I watched it live. There was about half an hour or so between this and the next video starting."

With a few touches to her iPhone and iPad, Madison started the next video.

"Okay and I'm back." Kate looked out from the screen. "The forensic guys made several calls to various experts in the field of working with mummies and said they're ready to remove the mummies. But I asked if I could get some more details, closer in video so that our team also gets a better in situ perspective. I mean, really, when archeologists and their teams make a find, everything is as thoroughly mapped, photographed, and graphed out as what forensic teams do. Maybe even more. So they said I can and that's what I'm going to do now."

Our view slowly panned to the dead men in the room Jebbin had fallen into.

CHAPTER 7

"I'LL ADMIT THIS IS GIVING ME THE WILLIES." THE SHAKINESS OF KATE'S voice backed up her words. "When I showed you all the photos of the mummies from when I was down here with Dr. Crawford, I'd stayed by the bed and used the zoom. I think for these to be more scientifically correct for the dig's records, I'm going to need to … be closer. One of the rescue team guys who'll be shoring up the roof when we're done has lent me his headlamp so I'll have good light for the closer photos.

"Okay. So, I'll … ah, start from here again and do a slow pan that we should then be able to break down into good, clear stills with a movie making program. I'm sure Ms. Walker has one. After that I'll move in closer to the … them. The forensic guys said they would share all the measurements they've taken with Dr. Koerner. Then we can use those and the stills pulled from my video to do a computer simulation of the room and the men."

Madison's head and mine were pressed together as we watched

the images of Kate panning on the iPad. I found myself wishing we were looking at this on a regular-sized laptop or even a desktop monitor. The video was good but I was sure we'd see more detail on a bigger screen.

Kate's voice continued on the video. "I'm starting at the door into the room, which is in the north wall of the room. The mummies are on the east side of the room. The forensic guys labeled this one Man A." She stopped on the desiccated man who was seated on the floor and leaning against the same wall the door was in. "I guess he's Man A because he's nearer the door into the room. And this guy …" She moved on to the man lying on his back on the floor. "He's B. If he was standing or sitting up, they'd be facing each other. I'll finish up my panning by returning to the bed. Okay. Done with that, now I'll move in closer starting with Man A."

The pale, leathery looking face of the mummified man filled the screen.

"He, ah, his skin isn't dark looking like I expected. He has a thick head of what looks like light brown hair and a beard and mustache that looks like something guys wear now, as you can see."

His beard went from loosely defined sideburns, along his jaw line with a line going up the center of his chin to his lower lip. The mustache was nicely shaped and did not extend beyond the corners of his mouth. Despite how disturbing he looked now (mummies usually disturb me), I had the feeling that he'd been quite dashing when he was alive.

The video image panned down his body.

"His shirt doesn't look too high-class, but nicer quality than I think a farmer would be wearing, so I'm thinking this one isn't Melvin Sutton since we know he was a sharecropper. You can see now where the hole in his shirt is although I don't expect it to line up with the actual wound since his body mass has decreased. Dark trousers, maybe wool or a wool blend, and rather normal looking boots. I'll move along to Man B."

Kate backed off a little and we saw the desk go by. It looked like there were some papers lying on it along with a book and a pair of oval wire-rimmed glasses. Just past the desk there were a few more papers on the floor along with a pen and spilt inkwell.

"Man B is on his back on the floor, partially on one of the throw rugs by the bed. His feet are nearest to me so I'll work my way up on him. Shoes are heavier boots than Man A was wearing. More like a farmer's work boots. Heavier weight pants in a more cotton-type fabric, I think. Coarser shirt. This is probably apt to be Melva's however-many-greats grandfather. I'm thinking we should get DNA from her and her dad as I'm pretty certain they can get some from the mummy. It'd be good for Melva and her dad to know whether or not one of the men was Melvin Sutton and which one of the mummies he was." Kate sighed, "It's gonna be rough on them either way.

"Um ... back to the details here. Again, you can see the hole where he was shot and again, I'm sure it doesn't line up with the wound. The, ah ... blood flowed a bit upward before going down his side. Perhaps because of the house being knocked off kilter." We heard her take a breath. "The faces do bother me. Ah. His skin is fairly light colored, like Man A. Man B has dark hair cut short with a beard. More neatly trimmed than Man A's—A's is more relaxed, artsy looking—ah, yeah, more neatly trimmed and only along the jaw line. No mustache. The blood has run toward the low side of the house, southward, and seemed to pool a lot in his armpit before soaking through his shirt enough to dribble along for a ways toward the wall. Coming around to show the bed on this side so we see where he is in relation to it and I'm done with the close-up video. Good timing, my battery is getting low, so I'll end this now. See you up top."

Madison shut off her iPad and phone while continuing the tale.

"She stayed until the forensic team finished up. The bodies were carefully wrapped and bagged and placed in the rescue basket, one at a time, then hoisted out. Just before the structural stabilization guys started to bolster the roof, the decision was made to bring Kate up. We all, I mean the dig team and me, we all moved the pavilion so it was over the hole. When the structural guys finished in the house they helped us cover the hole itself and sandbag a perimeter around the pavilion so we shouldn't get any water down the hole into the house." She grinned and corrected herself. "So you all shouldn't get any water in. I sorta keep forgetting that I'm not on the official crew."

I nodded, sighed, and sagged.

"You're worn out." Madison gave me a quick hug and stood up. "Are you staying here tonight?"

"Yes. Probably silly to do, but, you know, just in case he wakes up I want to be here."

"Not silly at all." She grabbed the back of the chair she'd brought in and started dragging it toward the door. "I'll have them bring in a cot for you." She stopped before she opened the door. "You're going to stick with the dig, aren't you? I mean … I know Dr. Crawford will need help with getting around and stuff, but are you going to go out to the dig too, right? This is really interesting and it'd be so cool to be able to help figure out what happened in the house. I'll drop some of my classes or something if you need me to … you know … be our eyes at the scene."

I walked over to her and hugged her tight. "We just can't resist getting our noses into everything, can we?" I held on but pulled back to look at her. "I plan to stick with the dig, though I may not be able to be there all day every day as I'd like to. Having you cover when I can't be there would be fantastic."

Her mood and reserve lifted. This time, she hugged me. "Awesome!" She broke the hug and reached for the doorknob. "Just let me know when you'll need me, and I'll say a prayer for you and

Dr. Crawford tonight. Night, Emory."

A few minutes later a nurse came in and we set up the portable bed. I stripped down to my camisole and undies—I wasn't going to get into bed in my filthy dig clothes—laid the oversize front-opening hospital gown she brought me to use as a bath robe over the end of Jebbin's bed, and lay down.

Yep. As soon as I did the phone in the room rang.

Molly and Freddy listened to my list of her father's injuries and my assurances that Jairus was making sure Jebbin and I would be well cared for. With obvious relief, they said they were glad to hear it, to keep them informed, and they would come over next week sometime after we'd had time to settle into our new routines.

I hung up. Lay down. Fell asleep.

And Lanthan and Felysse called. They got the same information. They said they'd call next week when we were settled into our new routines and we said our good nights.

After that, honestly, I don't remember a thing.

CHAPTER 8

FRIDAY CREPT IN WITH A DILUTED GREY DAWN. SOFT, STEADY RAIN—AN English sort of rain—dribbled slowly, with royal calmness, down the windowpanes of Jebbin's hospital room.

I had slept like I had been the one on pain meds. I'm sure nurses had come and gone, but I hadn't heard them. And yet ...

"Nurses, smurses, carry big purses," children's voices sing-songed in my head.

I came out of my doze and the children's voices faded away when Jebbin mumbled and moaned as he woke up.

Spiderman has his "Spidey Sense," I have my Wifey Sense. I was up, wondering what those children singing in my dream were doing at the nurses' station, putting on my makeshift bathrobe and next to my hubby's side so fast, it would have made Spiderman proud.

"Jebbin? You wakin' up, Hon?"

"Hmm?" His eyes stayed closed.

"Are you waking up?"

"I woke up a while ago. You were snorin'."

One blue eye opened, twinkling with mischief.

"Yeah, yeah. I'm sure I was. Smarty." I started rubbing his shoulder. "How are you feeling?"

"Uh. Okay. A little sore. Nurse said they were backing down a little on my pain meds to see how I do. So far, I do fine."

I gave him a kiss, which he happily returned in kind.

"Do you remember what happened yesterday?"

"Not sure, but I had this really weird dream about being in a dimly lit attic sort of place and there were a couple of mummy looking mannequins in there with me."

I reached for his right hand, the one that wasn't hurt, and shook it. "It wasn't a dream and let me be the first to congratulate you. You found the old Sutton House by falling through the roof."

His eyes widened and his lips parted in surprise. "I did what?"

"Fell through the roof and found the house. That's why you're here, Sweetie. It's how you got hurt."

He was silent for a moment. "And the mummies?"

"As I said, not a dream. We all figured that one of them is Melvin Sutton, but we really don't know for sure."

He exhaled. "Wow." He inhaled. "I gotta pee."

I wussed out. I pushed the call button and let a nurse help him. I reckoned I'd be doing enough of that once I took him home. No sense in my doing it here.

The nurse took a while to come out of the room. "I hope you didn't mind the wait, Mrs. Crawford." She had caught my attention as I was coming back down the hall. "I went ahead and took all his vitals and stuff since I was already in there."

"No trouble at all." I tugged the collar of my pseudo robe. "It isn't my favorite bathrobe, but it covers what needs covering."

We both laughed.

"At least it's a frontie, not a backie." She wiggled her brows.

"Thank goodness for small favors." I agreed. "How's my husband?"

"Really well. At least all his vitals are lookin' good, I should say. I don't know how anythin' else is coming along and I'd have to let the doctor fill you in on that information anyway. But yes, all the basics are lookin' good. Oh! He's gone back to sleep. Perfectly normal. His body has been through a lot and it's workin', workin', workin' at getting better. He's going to be sleepin' a lot over the next few days to a week or so."

"Thanks for reminding me. We've had all sorts of injuries and such down through the years, both us and our kids when they were still at home. Seems we all have a tendency to forget details like all the sleeping. But yes, I remember that."

I paused a moment as a thought formed in my head. I looked at my watch; it was 7:15.

"Actually, I think I'm going to call a friend to come get me and take me home for a few hours. I'll have to put my dirty clothes back on to go home, but I'm really sick and tired of being so grungy. Are you just starting your shift?"

"Yes, I am, and if he wakes up I'll let him know you went home to freshen up and will be back in a while."

"Thank you so much ... Betty." I had finally looked at her I.D. badge.

"No problem, Mrs. Crawford. You go home and get to feelin' more like yourself. He's not goin' anywhere."

I called AnnaMay. The library didn't open for another forty-five minutes, so there was plenty of time for her to drive me home. Once there, I'd have my own car again. I was waiting outside the main doors for her when she drove up and within ten minutes I was home.

The four-legged kids were obviously not happy. Confused would describe it better—just like any of us get when our routines have been overridden by something we don't really understand. Just like I was feeling, to be honest.

Sophie in particular was looking for Jebbin. She had welcomed me, but she kept looking at the door behind me. Her daddy and I had both left for longer than usual, at least without us packing suitcases ahead of time. How come we weren't both home? Hortense and Kumquat looked at me, intertwining with each other as they both circled, rubbing my ankles. Then they walked away. One of us was home and that was good enough for them.

I stripped off in the laundry room. No sense in dumping my dirty clothes in the bathroom where I'd only have to pick them up after I was all nice and clean. Straight into the washing machine they went. I'd wash them right after I finished my shower. I wasn't going to risk running out of hot water. I needed it more than the clothes did.

Thirty minutes later a cloud of steam preceded me out of the master bath. Oh the glorious feeling of being clean, after-bath oiled, and having clean, dry hair. I'd used my favorite citrusy shower gel to wash my hair as well as the rest of me, so all of me smelled zesty and fresh.

I gave the critters a light treat. A note on the bathroom mirror had informed me that Margery Purtle had come over to let Sophie out yesterday and this morning, scooped the litter boxes, and had given the kids their wet food treats last night and earlier this morning. I said a blessing for Marge and made myself a good eggs, wheat toast, bacon, and coffee breakfast, which I ate out on our screened porch.

While I ate, I booted up my laptop to check and clear out my emails.

There was lots of junk; there always is. Several emails had come from concerned friends who had heard about the accident on the local evening news—which made me wonder how much trouble Ceek would be having with gawkers and reporters. One email I was surprised to find was from Chatty, actually Dr. Nibodh Chatterjee, a forensic scientist friend of ours who runs a private forensics lab and occasionally comes to help Jebbin with cases.

> *Dear Emory,*
>
> *Jairus Twombly called yesterday to let me know what had happened to Jebbin and to report that he was amazingly well. I know he could have been injured to a much greater degree and rejoice that he was not.*
>
> *He also asked a favor that Deepti and I are honored to perform. Look for us to arrive at your home sometime later today, being Friday, along with our son, Ragesh. We have reserved a room at a local hotel so you do not need to be concerned about us being in your way. But Deepti will be at your home each day to assist in caring for Jebbin and to help with meal preparations, while I will be doing the forensic work on the mummies who were discovered in the buried house.*
>
> *You must not try to contact us to tell us not to come. We shall ignore you. We are, again, honored to be able to help.*
>
> *We look to be in Twombly by early afternoon and will call you at that time to see when it will be best to visit Jebbin in hospital and make further arrangements for helping you both.*
>
> *Until then, dearest Emory, we are yours faithfully,*
>
> *Chatty, Deepti, and Ragesh*
>
> *P.S. Ragesh will bring his violin with him. He wishes you to help him turn it into a fiddle.*

I was crying by the time I got to the postscript, which made me smile and laugh through my happy tears. Bless Jairus! Bless the Chatterjees! I was going to have help with Jebbin, Jebbin would not have to worry about who would cover the forensic work, and it was all happening with people we have fun being with.

I closed my eyes and sighed. Everything was going to be just fine.

CHAPTER 9

AH, THE JOY OF DRIVING MY LITTLE YELLOW BEETLE DOWN THE FAMILIAR road out to Sutton's Lake and the dig. Even though it had been raining since sometime last night, it had been a light rain, so I wasn't worried about the road being flooded out. I had the feeling that with the drop in the water level since the levee had broken, it would take a lot more rain to flood over this road again. What I didn't expect was a roadblock.

Two sawhorses with orange and white diagonal stripes effectively blocked each lane of the county road. A tarp canopy on the side of the road toward the lake kept the rain off two men, who, as I got closer, were revealed to be Oscar Hornsby and, oh joy, Sergeant Henry Schneider. Both men knew my car but only Henry got up to wait for me to pull even with them.

"Area's restricted, Mrs. Crawford." He was all business—and loathing. I hate to admit the feeling was mutual. "Dig team members only."

"She *is* dig team, Sergeant Schneider." Oscar's voice carried a smile I couldn't see with Henry blocking my view. "You are going to need to let her through."

The sergeant's eyes smoldered. "Ma'am," he said, touching the brim of his sheriff's hat. "Figures," was what I heard, as he turned aside to move the nearest barricade.

I winked at Oscar, who was chuckling, as I drove through. I parked behind Ronnie's car. She and Mack came out to the dig together every day. Jebbin and I had a feeling they had more going on than just the dig, but if they did, they had been pretty discreet while on the site. By the time I got to the pavilion, my shoes were heavy with mud.

The south and east sides of the pavilion were tied up like tent flaps to get some air under there. The slight breeze was blowing the rain from the northwest. Those two sides were down tight. The team was in the pavilion, where the hole in the roof was protected from the elements. Since Ceek had us start at 6:00 each morning, they had been here for about three and a half hours today.

"Emory!" Nancy called out, and then she snapped a photo of me. "How's Jebbin?"

I was soon surrounded by the team all asking the same question.

"He's as fine as he can be," I informed them. "A bit high on pain meds, so it's kind of hard to tell."

"Is he going to be able to come back?" Ceek asked.

I was surprised Ceek wasn't down in the house.

"I tend to doubt it," I answered. "But I guess one never knows. He has a broken right heel, a severely sprained left wrist, and a lot of other sprains, strains, and pulled things. He'll probably be in a wheelchair for several weeks since he can't put weight on his injured wrist." I made like I was supporting myself on crutches. "That cancels out crutches until the wrist heals really well. I don't think we'd have much luck getting him across all the soft sandy or muddy ground to get over here." I looked at the opening to the house. "Why are you up top, Ceek?"

"We're trying to have only two of us at a time in the house until it's more thoroughly assessed," he explained. "The structural guys who work with rescue teams are good, but they can't do a full inspection or shore things up in a more permanent manner. They are trained for doing what needs to be done to get people out of collapsing buildings, caves, or sewers. Those sorts of things. I want the house looked at by a structural engineer and to have necessary support repairs done by experienced carpenters who won't ruin the historical integrity of the house just to strengthen it."

I nodded. "Makes sense. So," I looked around. "Dan and Hank are in the house checking out its design and structure?"

It was then I noticed Madison and Melva standing at the edge of the group. Madison was looking back at me. I gave her a nod, which she returned. We'd talk later. Melva was looking at the ground, out the open side of the pavilion, up at the plastic over her head—anywhere other than at Ceek or myself. I was relieved to see her here; it meant she hadn't done anything too drastic when she left The Coal Bin yesterday after blowing up at her dad. From her body language I could sense a bad mood coming off her like heat waves off summer blacktop. Hopefully she would be willing to talk to me later as well.

"Yes." Ceek answered my question. "They did holler up a while ago to say that it seemed like an odd design for a house in that era. The top level is a half story, which was not common for farmhouses back then. If they bothered with an upstairs, it was usually either a full second floor or they would only have a loft across one end of the home. The guys have determined there's a four-foot wall all the way around the second floor, with the sloped ceilings going up from there. Other than the half-story, it's a basic American Foursquare design house with a hipped roof. With that style the edge of the roof is even all the way around and often has a foot-and-a-half to two-foot overhang. We think that's how the sink hole got capped and the house was preserved.

"I told the team when they first got here that I came early this morning with Richard Freeman, a geologist friend of mine, and we looked at the earth that's pressed against the windows. He pointed out smears of something white running vertically in the soil along with wood splinters. He thought the white might be whitewash. It doesn't look heavy enough to be paint. Considering the splinters that are mixed in, he said he suspects the house fell into a sink hole that was a surprisingly tight fit."

With a small flick of his hand Ceek indicated a worktable in one corner of the pavilion.

"Everyone else has seen this already but you're all welcome to have a look at it again or get started figuring out where the outline of the house is."

Everyone went off to get to work, some still inside the pavilion and some out in the rain, but Melva and Madison followed us to the table.

"Both of us got here after he'd told everyone about this." Madison explained while Melva said nothing and kept her eyes averted.

Ceek grabbed a sketchpad and showed us a drawing of a house with a low-pitched roof, the surface of the ground the roof was resting on, and a hole that had formed under it. There was also a cutaway view that illustrated the amount of roof overhang.

"Richard figured the soil scraped the walls of the house as it fell." Ceek pointed to the larger view. "The hipped roof on an American Foursquare looks like someone set a pyramid on top of the four exterior walls. The roof's overhang, the eaves, like I said before are completely even on all sides of the house—unlike a two-sided peaked roof which isn't even—you know—two of the exterior walls go straight up into the peak of the roof forming triangle shapes." He circled around the cutaway view with his finger. "The wide eaves all on the same level capped off the hole tight enough that very little water from the actual flood got in around the walls. Then the silt some of you thought had buried the entire house only had to cover over the roof. That's why, even after everything settled and the water in the new lake had cleared, nobody ever saw the house."

"Whoa!" Melva gasped. Sometime while Ceek was showing the drawings she must have decided to look as well as listen.

"That's cool!" That was Madison.

"Wouldn't it have busted up?" was my contribution.

Ceek held up his hands to silence us. "I know. It seems an outrageous theory, but Richard assured me that it's entirely possible. He said sinkholes can be as weird as tornados. He's seen houses split nearly clean in half with one half in the hole and the other sitting up on top with most of the furniture still in place. And he's seen whole buildings that are nothing but rubble at the bottom of the hole. He wants to do some more evaluating, you know, get ahold of some of the big boy toys that geologists use that aren't in our budget—a magnetometer, a ground-penetrating radar unit—and do some more looking underneath the house and at the ground surrounding it."

The four of us at the table turned simultaneously to look at the hole with the ladder sticking out as though it was blowing a raspberry at us. We just stood there. Even if the sinkhole theory proved right, which I thought it would, knowing how it happened wouldn't make the whole situation feel any less strange and mysterious. Not with the two mummies inside. I felt the tingle of my intuition. I needed to find out the story of it all.

The eerie moment passed. The tableau broke.

"Can the three of us go down?" Madison, all enthusiasm and energy, grabbed three strong flashlights off a nearby table, handed one each to Melva and me, and was already heading toward the ladder. "We're keeping Dr. Crawford informed about the dig, so he won't feel totally left out of the adventure."

"Ah, yeah." Ceek came out of his reverie. "Yeah. Why not? Go on down, but we're staying on the second floor for now. Clean as much of the mud off your shoes as you can first."

"Will do, Dr. Koerner." She availed herself of the boot scraper someone had set beside the ladder then started down. "Come on, you guys."

Melva and I headed for the scraper and ladder.

"Emory."

"Yes?" I paused to look over at Ceek, and then went back to thoroughly scraping my shoes.

"I think the rest of us will break for lunch while you all have your look around. And keep an eye on those two. I don't think Melva will damage anything but I'm really having trouble getting a read on her. And sometimes Madison's enthusiasm scares me a little." Ceek winked at me as I swung myself onto the ladder.

"Me, too." I grinned back. "See you all in a bit."

Then I stepped onto the ladder and down into the sunken house for the first time.

CHAPTER 10

AS I CLIMBED DOWN, A DISQUIETING FEELING CAME OVER ME.

A strange, unique feeling.

Each rung down seemed to be a step further back in time.

The air was heavy, even though it had none of the moist dampness of the air up under the pavilion. It was surprisingly dry, even now with it open to the surface air, like some basements I've been in. And like those basements, even though dry, it still had that underground smell. It was mustiness without a true dampness at its source. Psychosomatic? Maybe. Perhaps just knowing one is underground sets the brain free to experience all the odors and sensations it associates with basements or caves. Either way, it was unsettling.

Upon reaching the bare wood floor, I turned my back to the ladder and looked around. Madison was already nosing about the bedroom. Melva was nowhere to be seen, which worried me a little. For the moment I wanted to stay in one place and take it all in.

"Melva?" I called out.

"I'm being good," she called back, annoyance clear in her tone. "I'm checking out the layout and the other bedrooms. I'm not going downstairs," then with a nasty little chuckle, she added, "yet."

My years of mom-hood let me know my chain was being yanked. "Just wanted to know you hadn't fallen through the floor or anything."

The team had run electricity into the room from a generator on the surface. They'd put an incongruous, completely modern looking torchiere-style floor lamp at the foot of the bed where the ceiling was the highest. It looked so wrong but illuminated the room nicely. I left the flashlight Madison had handed me in my pocket.

The dust on the floor was marked with scuffs from the paper booties the forensic team wanted everyone to wear while they did their work, along with Dan and Hank's shoe prints. The bed where Jebbin had landed was on my right and overhead was the part of the hole where he'd actually dropped through, not where it had been enlarged so they could get him out. They'd enlarged the one side so we all wouldn't have to walk on the shattered remains of the bed.

The hole.

In the ceiling.

In the roof.

Where Jebbin had fallen through into this walk-in time capsule.

I looked up over my shoulder. It was easy to see that the sloped ceiling was only the width of the joists away from the underside of the roof, and the ceiling itself was only thin lath and plaster. The joists must have been further apart than usual in modern construction, or rotten; otherwise, Jebbin would probably have gotten stuck part way instead of falling clean through. About a foot in from the end of the bed, the ceiling quit following the slope of the roof and had been built to level off at about seven feet from the floor instead of going up into the point of the roof. I could see places all over the ceiling where plaster had fallen away from the lath to lay in broken, dusty piles on the floor and furniture.

The small table we'd seen in the video, maybe Polly Sutton's dressing table, was to my left in front of the window that looked out onto …

For a moment, my spine tingling, I could see what Polly most likely had seen. Farm fields of wheat or hay swaying in a prairie breeze under the summer sun, heading west up the slope of the ridge that ran north and south about a half mile up the road.

The vision vanished. There was nothing now. Only earth pressed tight against the glass. Tight against the walls. Burying the roof.

I shook myself. I'm not normally bothered by closed-in spaces—I often enjoy them—but there was something about this place …

I had just noticed the gingham curtains, now grey with dust and cobwebs, that framed the dead window and I was taking a step toward the tipped-over wardrobe when I stumbled, slapping my hand onto Polly's table to catch myself.

"Are you okay?" Madison asked from the opposite side of the room.

"Yeah. Yes, I'm all right. The room feels so … off, and I know why. I forgot what Kate said about it being out of alignment. I lost my balance a little because the floor was closer than I expected. It's uphill going this way."

"I noticed, but I didn't lose my balance over it," she teased.

"Only because you're a child," I chided her in return. "Children don't lose their balance. Didn't you know that?"

We laughed as I wiped the dust from the table off my hand.

"More like it was because I wasn't watching where I was going. I was looking out the window."

"Looking out …" Madison looked behind me at the dark window but left it at that.

I looked behind me at the short half-wall of the room that would be facing the lake, specifically to where it met the sloped ceiling. "Look at that!" I pointed where I was looking. "Look at that gap along the top of the south wall."

"Wow!" Melva was back in the room. She took a couple steps closer to the back wall then looked side to side along its length. "The wall and the ceiling don't meet at all along the whole south side. And look there, and there!" Her outstretched finger followed the lines of the west and then the east walls. They also sported gaps where they should have met the ceiling.

We all tracked the gap. It was close to six inches wide across the south wall.

"And look," I added. "There are cracks in the side walls."

The gap was only about an inch narrower by the time the side walls reached the north wall of the room.

After a few moments of contemplation, Madison spoke. "I'm sure Dan and Hank noticed all this, but we should mention it all the same."

I nodded. "I agree."

Melva inhaled sharply. "You guys want to go look at the rest of the house?" came out with her exhale.

"Sounds good to me, but we're only supposed to be upstairs, remember."

Looking heavenward, she sighed. "Yes, Emory." Then she dashed out the door. "I'll beat-cha!" she added as though the rest of the bedrooms were far away.

The door opened onto a hallway that ran from one side of the house to the other. On the right, to the east, were the stairs. On the left the hall ended at a brick wall that was most likely the chimney for the huge fireplace homes in those days would have on the main floor. To the right of the chimney there was a curtain that was the height of the wall and about three or four feet wide. I reckoned it was most likely storage space of some sort. On the same side as the curtain were two doors that Dan and Hank must have propped open; the slant of the house would have held them closed. Lots of scuffing in the dust on the floor made it clear others on the team had already checked out the rooms. Melva and Madison ducked into the furthest one while I moseyed into the closer one and pulled out my flashlight.

The room was plain and small. To the right of the door was a set of narrow bunk beds stripped to the blue-and-white striped ticking of the mattress. Across the room along the far wall was a slightly wider bed. I trailed my fingers along the stripes to feel the coarse fabric through the dust, which wasn't as heavy in this room as it was in the master bedroom where the damage to the house was worse. I thought about the Suttons. There were two older boys from Melvin's first marriage and two younger ones he'd had with Polly. The older boys, who were in their mid to late teens, probably had the bunks, while the younger boys shared the wider bed.

Another dark window, reflecting back the glow from my flashlight, was in the far wall at the foot of the younger boys' bed. Pegs and a couple of shelves on the wall across from the bunks accounted for all the storage the boys had in their room. The beds were stripped and the room empty of personal items because Melvin Sutton had sent his family off, up to Polly's kin folk up near Xanthe, north between Twombly and Bloomington.

I chuckled. An odd thought occurred to me and I got on my knees to look under the beds.

Yes.

The chamber pots were still there. Hopefully they'd been emptied before Polly and the children left, but I wasn't going to check it out. I did want to check out some other things the flashlight showed under there.

"Madison or Melva." I hollered.

"Yes?" Unison voices replied.

"I was wondering …"

A scuffing noise made me turn. I turned to see both girls in the doorway, their clothes all dusty and each clutching something in their hands.

"I *was* wondering if you'd be willing to crawl under the beds but your clothes answer that question. I spotted some things under there," I gestured toward their hands, "as it appears you did in the other room. Have at it." I waved toward the dark spaces as I got out of the way.

They both looked about for a moment before shoving the things in their hands on top of the top bunk. "No peaking," Melva ordered then practically dove under the bunk beds and disappeared from view. "Mine either." Madison shook her finger at me before diving under the younger boys' bed. I followed the glow of their flashlights and the sound of them scooting about on the floor. Chamber pots appeared from under the foot of each bed followed by the two freshly dust-covered girls with their flashlights clenched in their teeth and a few grimy items in their hands.

"It's like the stuff I found in what must have been their daughters' room next door," Madison said. "Empty chamber pots and a few items that had probably been lost under the beds before they left. We took photos with our phones so we'd know where everything was."

"I can't believe you two looked in the chamber pots! Ewww!" I scrunched up my face in disgust and then laughed.

The girls looked at each other and shrugged.

"We figured anything in them was way past being smelly by now," Melva said.

They both folded up the fronts of their T-shirts and put the things from under the boys' beds and the things they'd put on the top bunk in the makeshift pouches, and then we went back into the master bedroom where the light was better.

Madison turned to Melva.

"I always heard that Mrs. Sutton and the kids all went up near Xanthe. Is that what your family says?"

"Yes," Melva answered softly. "Polly and the children left a few days before the big flood, when I'm sure they had time to pack carefully. Not that they would have had many belongings anyway. To be honest," she looked around the room, "I'm surprised this is as nice a house as it is. According to everything I've read, they were sharecroppers, and sharecroppers usually got low-grade housing."

Madison started to put the things they'd found on the desk but Melva put out a hand to stop her.

Melva looked at both of us. "I know this is going to sound awful," she said in a whisper, "but I'd rather keep these to ourselves for a little bit. Otherwise we have to hand them over to Dr. Koerner, and I don't know how much of a chance we'll have to really look them over. I've got lots of pockets. Can we just take them with us and sneak them back later? I mean, in a way, they kinda belong to me anyway seeing as I'm a Sutton."

It was my turn to hesitate.

Her eyes looked sad. "Can we?"

I'm a responsible adult.

A pastor's daughter.

A mother.

But I *had* been thinking exactly the same thing as the hurting young lady next to me.

"I'm most likely going to regret this," I whispered back, "but yes. And let's look behind those curtains in the hall and under the mattress in here. We can check under the desk and look in its drawers, too, but I think we'll have to pass on the wardrobe." I waved my hand at the large tipped over piece of furniture. "I don't think we can lift it without making too much noise. I don't see what harm it can do. I mean Dr. Koerner technically *has* what he was looking for. He was after the house and we found the house. He's even pretty sure he knows how it managed to disappear without a trace."

"I know," Madison said as she and Melva headed back into the hallway. "The rest is just icing to him." She paused in the doorway and turned to me with a huge smile. "We have a mystery to solve."

Ten minutes later we were back up the ladder, bid farewell to the rest of the crew, and headed to our various homes to get cleaned up. At least, that's what we told them.

And no one said a thing about our bulging pockets.

CHAPTER 11

MADISON TWOMBLY SAT AT MY KITCHEN TABLE WRAPPED IN THE GUEST bathrobe I keep in my linen closet. Melva Suter sat across from her wearing my own chenille robe, which wrapped around her completely, so that the opening was almost in the back instead just off to the left side.

I'm pudgy but not *that* pudgy, it's just that Melva is so thin.

I'd changed into clean jeans and a T-shirt since it was my house and I had all my clothes available to me. The clothes we'd had on at the dig had gone through a short cycle in the washing machine and were now in the dryer. Spread across the table were the sandwiches, chips, deli dill pickles, and cookies we'd picked up from Jimmy John's, the things we'd found at the Sutton House that we'd stuffed in our pockets and under our shirts ... and two curious cats. Kumquat and Hortense were behaving themselves only because they had their favorite kitty treats to make our food less interesting and they appeared to find the items from the house either too horrible-smelling to bother with, or just too dusty to be appealing.

Silly cats don't know real treasure when they smell it.

"Looks interesting," I said as we started sorting things out. We had placed them all in an empty Walmart bag when we got to my car.

"I know. It's a lot more than I expected to find. This goes in the boys' room pile." Melva placed the larger of two dolls into the boys' pile. "Not sure what they were doing with a dolly but it was all the way back in the hardest corner to get to under the big bed."

"One of the younger brothers must have snitched it to tease one of his sisters." Madison chuckled. "I doubt if the two older boys would have done it."

I laughed. "Spoken like a girl with an older brother."

"Oh yeah." She gave us a knowing smile.

"I don't suppose the stuff from the kids' rooms will be much help with figuring out what happened with the guys in the parents' room," Melva said as she nabbed a yo-yo from the jumble and set it with the boys' stuff.

"There wasn't anything in the cupboard out in the hall except stuff that was too big to sneak out with. I do think we hit pay dirt in the parents' room." Madison had checked behind the curtain in the hall since it was just past the door into the girls' room.

The boys' room had produced a couple of small hand-carved wooden soldiers and a small wooden horse of matching size that was missing a front leg. We also had the yo-yo, four marbles, one domino, and the aforementioned larger sized cloth dolly. There was also a partially used pack of cigarette papers, which I was hoping had been used by the eldest boy, not the younger ones.

Madison had found a few hair ribbons in the girls' room along with a comb with missing teeth, a smaller dolly than the one in the boys' room, a tiny chair—most likely from a doll house, a cup and ball toy, and a length of yarn tied in a loop.

"No," I replied as I picked up the two dollies. "I don't think any of this will help solve our cold case. But these dolls explain something to me."

"What's that?" Melva said as both girls leaned in for a closer look.

"Notice how well they're made? All hand sewn. Delicate embroidered facial features. Simple but sweet little dresses." I sat the smaller doll on the tiny chair. "And made so they can sit down. Part of the story of the Sutton House was that Polly went into business as a seamstress after the tragedy, and now I believe it."

Melva picked up the bigger doll, handling it with caring gentleness. "Wow. This is well made. And to think my great-great-great-grandmother made it all by hand. She's what, about eight inches tall? Obviously not part of a doll house, unless the girls wanted to pretend she was a giant." Her voice sounded dreamy as she danced the doll gracefully from side to side. "Maybe a giant's daughter."

Madison picked up the smaller doll. I watched as they danced the dolls around the piles of memories on my kitchen table and a knowin' came over me as I did. Madison was touched by the care put into the tiny handmade doll. She had never known a simple life like the little girl whose doll she held. Even though, as far as I knew, the Twombly family had always raised their children to be as down to earth as possible, it is still very different when you're a child of the richest family in a small town.

Melva lived in the age of electricity and electronic gadgetry. She'd had comforts beyond the imaginations of the farm girls she was distantly related to. But, I sensed that as those long ago girls had, Melva had lived a hard life. She had worked at her family's restaurant since she was little and had lost her mother when still a child. Yet I smiled at the soft smile on her face and the gentle way she moved the bigger doll. The doll moved like the accomplished dancer who controlled her had once moved—pirouetting high on her toes and leaping gracefully over objects that had strayed from the piles.

Strangely in unison, the dolls stopped dancing. The twenty-first century girls came back to the now.

"Well, or maybe not a giant's daughter. I'm not sure a giant's daughter would have been so graceful." Madison reached for the little wooden chair and sat her dolly in it. "Would you mind if I keep her, Melva? There's an old dollhouse in the attic at Cornelia House. I've wanted an excuse to bring it down and clean it up. I think she might like it."

"Yeah, sure. Why not?" Melva looked at me. "That is, if it's okay that we keep any of this stuff."

"I don't think it will matter at all." And to be honest, I didn't care if it did. The way the dolls had touched these girls' hearts was worth any hassle keeping them might cause.

"Cool!" Madison smiled and started to put the small doll and chair in her pocket. "Oops. Better wait till I've got my clothes back on instead of this bathrobe. And probably best not to just stuff her and her chair in a pocket again. I kinda keep forgetting how old they are." She set the toys aside, away from the other stuff, and then leaned across the table toward me. "Alright, your turn, old sleuthing partner. We've got to have a look at the books you found in the bedroom."

I leaned in toward her. "Nope. Best for last. Let's look at the three coins first, then the watch, the piece of paper and the writing supplies, and then the books." I'd grabbed all these from Melvin and Polly's room. I'd decided to leave the things that were on the desktop, though, thinking it would be too noticeable to the rest of the dig team if the desk was suddenly cleared off. A ceramic candlestick holder had stood on the desk with a candle in it that was burnt down as far as it would go. There were also two pieces of similarly burnt-down candles that must have been dug out of the holder and an empty matchbox. It had all somehow managed to stay on the desk when the house sank and went out of plumb.

The coins had been under the bed, the last stuff we'd found.

Madison and I had held up the mattress while Melva took photos and then grabbed the coins.

Melva flopped back in her chair with a huff. "Okay. I know I'm just a hanger-on-er here, but really? We start with the coins?"

Madison snatched them up off the table before we could stop her. "Alrighty. I'll just have a look at them and get them out of our way, shall I?" She spread them out on her palm. "We've got one, ah …" She flipped over the smallest coin, looking for the date, I assumed. "One 1838 half-dime. Precursor to the nickel, though for a while they minted both. Slightly smaller than the modern nickel but bigger than our current dime."

I sat there with my mouth hanging open. I had expected a cutesy comment like "*There, I looked at them,*" rather than the informed answer I had just gotten.

"What?" She gave me a smug smile. "You didn't know that, oh *wise older* partner? I guess I forgot to tell you that for three years, when I was nine, ten, and eleven, I was a member of the Springfield Junior Numismatists Club. Next coin. An 1841 half-cent, you know, a carry over from when we were British and had their ha-penny. We hung onto having a half-cent coin for sixty-four years before we decided to chuck it."

"It's huge. You sure it's a half penny?" Melva peered at the large copper coin.

"Yep." Madison turned it over to show the words 'HALF CENT' on the reverse side. "I know. I always thought it was weird, too, that a half penny would be so big. Then last, we have an 1843 quarter, or a two-bit piece as in 'shave and a haircut, two bits,'" she sang the old ditty. "Okay. All done with the coins." Madison looked at me and quirked an eyebrow—I knew what she was asking and gave a slight nod. She took hold of Melva's hand, turned it palm up, dropped the coins onto her palm and closed her fingers over them. "You might want to look into the value of the half-cent and the half-dime, Melva.

They may be worth quite a bit of money."

Then Madison sat up straight with her hands clasped on the table in front of her, looking all prim, proper, and attentive.

"Now, your turn, Mrs. Crawford. The watch and the book, if you don't mind, and you'd better not spend much time on the watch."

I picked up the watch. It was amazingly dust free. I suppose with no movement in the master bedroom until Jebbin fell in, the dust that settled everywhere else didn't get very far under the bigger pieces of furniture. Since the books, the paper with the writing, and the watch might be important clues, I had taken photos of them all with my phone. I also took several photos of the things I left on the desktop.

"This looks expensive," I muttered while turning it over in my hands. "It has Agassiz & Compagnie on the face." I looked up at Madison. "Which I've never heard of, so I can't look smug." We all laughed and I went on. "I would say it's gold, not brass, and, as you can also see, it's beautifully engraved, or stamped, or however they would have done all that decorative stuff around the edges. Let me see if I can pop it open." I tried for a bit using my thumbnail then got a small pocketknife from my tool drawer in the kitchen and finally pried it open.

"There's an inscription. Okay, this is good. It isn't Melvin Sutton's."

"Why is it good that it isn't Melvin's?" Melva asked. The girls came around to my side of the table to look over my shoulder at the inscription.

"Oh! I didn't mean it that way." I laughed. "I meant good, there's an inscription, and they aren't Melvin's initials so it can't be his."

"*To R.L.W. from Father.*" Madison read aloud. "Do you have any idea who that could be?"

For a few moments I just sat there. I felt that I should know who that was from all the reading that I had done about the incident, and I was sure that if I had the first or last name I would, but with just the initials, nothing was coming to me.

"No, I don't. But I'd be willing to bet that one of the mummies is R.L.W. and the other is Melvin Sutton. I found it under the desk, but sort of in the middle, not really closer to one or the other man."

The girls moved back to their seats as Madison said, "That sounds like good thinking to me. Although I wonder how the watch got under the desk. It's not something someone would just toss aside."

"Most likely we'll never know the answer to that." I closed up the watch and looked up at her. "I don't suppose I should open one of the books?"

"'Bout time." Melva huffed as she sat down, but then smiled.

I set the watch to one side and took up the biggest book. It was about twelve inches tall, eight inches wide, an inch thick, and had a red book cloth cover with a gold-embossed pattern on the front that reminded me of the top faceting on a rectangle-shaped gemstone.

"I didn't take the time to look them over, I just grabbed stuff. If you recall, the desk was open like a simple table to the left, with one drawer about a foot wide and half that deep with a cabinet with a door below it on the right. This," I waggled it for emphasis, "was in the drawer. There's nothing distinguishing about the cover." I turned it to look at the spine. "Oh! It's a ledger."

I carefully opened the thick book and looked down the column of entries.

"It's for the farm business. This is a fairly good quality book; the cover and the binding are in good shape. I'm thinking Melvin was supplied this by the landowner since these records would have been important to him." I looked at it a few more seconds then shut the ledger. "I have one of my feelings that while this could be a fascinating read, I don't think this will tell us much about what happened between the two men. Let's move on."

Melva fixed me with a quizzical stare. "One of your 'feelings?'"

"Yes. Ah. It's a really strong intuition sort of thing. Both my grannies got 'feelings' about things and I do too, though I used to ignore it as best I could. I've been learning to listen to them more in the last year."

She grunted an unconvinced monosyllable then gave me an order. "Next book."

"Okay," I replied and picked up the middle-sized book that was around eight-by-ten inches and half an inch thick. "This was resting on its spine up against the back of the cabinet behind a stack of newspapers that covered it from easy view. If I hadn't been specifically looking for hidden things, I wouldn't have found it."

The girls leaned in again.

"That sounds more promising," Madison said.

The cover was in tones of browns, oranges, and golds, and looked like a cross section of a cement block full of different pebble sized irregular shapes against, in this case, a deep-orangey background.

"It's not in as good a shape as the ledger. Probably a cheaper book," I said as I opened it up.

CHAPTER 12

THERE WAS NO BLANK FLYLEAF OR A TITLE PAGE. IT WENT STRAIGHT TO a page full of handwriting with a date at the top.

"I think it's a diary," I whispered.

"I know people don't want anyone looking at their diaries," Madison observed, "but that seems a kinda weird place to hide one."

"Seeing it was in the desk, are you thinking it was Grandpa Melvin's?" Melva was gently touching the book with her index finger.

"I don't think it's the usual kind of diary. It sounds like someone else was supposed to read it. Let me read the first entry to you."

I cleared my throat and started.

Monday 15th May, 1843

Jr., Emmett and me found the place we are goin to start the job from. There be a small rise that is well treed north of the road by near to 50 yards and then west bout quarter mile. Goin west is uphill from here as tis. That n the rise should keep it dry even if we get a wetter n usual season. There is timber in the stand that we can use of bracing when we run out of what I have.

Ya had said ya wanted the entrnce off your land. This is. Yet close enough that we when we start digging will not have far to get inta your land.

Will start tonight n hope to get well along enough that will be out a folks sight from then on. Will put the details in here like ya said to.

⌒

"Grandpa's definitely talking to someone else," Melva said after we had all sat quietly for a moment. "It sounds like he took on extra work of some kind other than the farming."

"We should see if we can find where he's talking about." Madison was into her perky detective mode. "Sounds to me like they were digging some kinda tunnel since he mentions digging and needing lumber for bracing."

Before I could say anything Melva cut in.

"No. I … ah, don't see any need to do that. We need to be finding out who the guys in the house are and if we can … um, figure out what happened in there. I want to know if one of them really is Grandpa Melvin and if one is him, then who is the guy who shot him?" She paused, then in a lighter tone said, "Let's see what the last book is."

I was surprised by Melva's interjection. I would have said she'd jump at this opportunity. Once again my back and neck were tingling. Something about what the diary entry described was important to her but I felt this wasn't the time to press the girl about it.

"Okay," was all I said. Melva sighed, sounding relieved, and looked down at the table. I flicked a glance over at Madison who caught my meaning.

"Do you think it's Polly's?" Madison cheerily asked as I picked up the four-by-six-inch book covered with lightweight cotton fabric in a blue and white plaid.

"Yes," I happily confirmed. "I would think so. We know she loved fabric arts and sewing. I can imagine her buying a very inexpensive little pocketbook and covering it with cloth of her choosing."

I undid the button and tab fastening and opened the cover to reveal the hand stitching that shaped the cover and the tension threads that kept it taut. I pointed to the opposite page where a neat hand had written *The Diary of Polly Sutton for the year 1843.* Below that she had added *and part of 1844.*

"Why would she leave her diary behind?" Melva asked.

"It had fallen between the wall and a leg of her table. I think it got knocked off the table and its absence wasn't noticed when she packed her things. Which makes me wonder …"

I turned to the back of the small book, then back a few pages until I found a dated page.

"The house disappeared on July sixth. They later found out that Polly and the children had left three days before, so that'd be July third." I pointed to the date on the page. "You can see this is dated July second and it's the last entry because the book is full. I assume she started a new book."

"I get it," Madison said. "Like she had already packed up the new one and probably meant to add the old one to her things before they left in the morning. But somehow, this managed to fall behind the table in between times."

"Sounds quite likely, Madison. A very good theory about another mystery I'm sure we won't be able to solve." I laughed and then took a drink of my soda from Jimmy John's to wet my whistle. "Let's see what Polly had to say her last night in her home."

I began to read the July second entry.

Dear Diary,   *July 2, 1844*

Well, the youngins and I leave tomorrow morning after chores. I would not feel right leaving without helping Melvin with the chores.

I'm not happy to be leaving at all, truth be told. Melvin seems to think that the flooding will be gettin worse and wants us to leave while the ford is passible. I think that tis awfully late in the season and that the weather should be turnin hotter and dryer. But he is insisting.

Somethins going on with him, I'm thinkin. He has been insisting about a lot of things of late. He's been changing. Getting in a tizzy over things that ought not to bother him. Been doing it for nearly a year, though it has been gettin worse the last few months and specially since the flooding has been so bad. Him, Junior, Emmett and even young Horace. They rush through the work on this place then hurry off somewheres to help some neighbors hereabouts. But they don't tell me which neighbors and they head off ta the northwest where the nearest neighbor is a couple of miles off. And they come home of the evenin filthy from the tops of their heads down, a whole lot dirtier than farming usually gets a person. I'm wonderin when mister R. will be raisein a stink over it. Maybe he taint found out yet that my men folk keep galivantin off to other folks farms.

Melvin told us to pack most all our things. Told me last night it is to not loose much to the floodin. I think it is more to do with the creaking and shimmyin the house has been doing the last few weeks. Not to awful bad, but I have noticed. Maybe Melvin is thinking there is gonna be an earthquake like the New Madrid one thirty some years back and just sayin it's because of the floods. There's folks round here that still talk about that. Even though we don't speak of such in front of the little ones, I'm thinking they are not believing us that we just be going to their Uncle and Aunt's farm for a visit. We don't usually take so much with us when we go visitin. The older boys want to stay but Melvin said no. Just in case we get stuck somewheres he wants them with the youngins and me to unstick the wagon or unhitch the horses and ride for help.

I had best be closing this entry. I got myself a new diary book all bought and in my satchel downstairs. I'll stick you in there in the morning.

Polly

We were all quiet for a few moments, thinking over what I'd read.

"Well, my theory was right." Madison was contemplative, not crowing as I expected. "One mystery solved. She did mean to take this with her."

"I wonder if there was an earthquake?" Melva sounded sad. "Maybe that's what caused the sink hole and made the house sink."

"You'd think it would have affected more than just that house, though. And then we have a 'mister R.' in Polly's letter, and R.L.W. on the watch. I think we have a clue as to who either mummy A or mummy B is. Whoever he is, he may have been at the house to 'raise a stink' about it like Polly feared and it got out of hand."

I looked at the kitchen clock. "I think we need to get you two dressed and you, Melva, back to the dig and Madison to Cornelia House. The team is set to go down to the main floor of the house and Madison and I will need a report." I winked and smiled at Melva and she winked back. "I'm going to have company sometime this afternoon or evening, and I want to get back to the hospital. I'm wondering how my good man is doing."

"Papa told me he was contacting the Chatterjees about coming to help you and Dr. Crawford," Madison said as they stood up. "Are they the company? Oh, and can you take me to Willow Creek? I have my mandolin lesson this afternoon and the subdivision is out near Sutton's Lake. I'll just hang out at Mrs. Patterson's house."

"Yes, it's the Chatterjees and sure, I'll take you over to the Patterson's." I smiled and waved the girls toward the laundry room. "Go get dressed."

Madison hung back next to me as Melva went into the laundry room to get her clothes.

"I said that about my lesson 'cause I need to talk to you," she rattled off fast then dashed down the short hall.

I had wondered about that as I knew her lessons were at the Patterson's Music Store, not at their home.

With Madison in the front seat and Melva in the back we headed off to the dig site. We went through the checkpoint near the dig, stopped along the road opposite the pavilion to drop Melva off, then headed west to Willow Creek road and turned right, which would take us where we could double back to Twombly.

I kept waiting for her to start talking, but when we'd arrived at the outskirts of town and she hadn't said a word, I reckoned I'd better.

"Okay, what's up?"

"I, ah … I just wanted to tell you there's one of those parties I mentioned to you before. It's … ah, happening tonight and I'm going."

She was talking too fast for me to interrupt.

"My best friend Diane and her older brother, Doug, are going too. Doug's driving since Diane and I can't yet. So I won't be alone. We've already planned it all out. We will stay together and not drink anything anyone offers us. Doug doesn't drink at all, even though he's old enough to, so that's all good with him being our driver. I'll check out everything I can and let you know what I find out," she rushed on. "I'm taking a little test-tube with a stopper in case I get a chance to snag a sample of the booze the kids are all talking about."

We weren't yet to Cornelia House but I pulled to the curb, put on the parking brake, and turned to face Madison. "What gave you this lame-brained idea?" She had the same stubborn look on her face that her father gets.

"I told you I was going to check into the parties and the super booze I keep hearing about. How else am I supposed to do that?"

Did I hear a defensive note in her voice? Her chin was now jutting out in 'rebellious mode.' "I don't know, Miss Tech Expert. I would have thought you'd figure something out." I looked out the windshield. "I have to tell your parents."

"No!"

"You're a minor, and …"

"Emory, please. *No.* We've made good plans. There will be three of us, we stay together and we are taking our own water bottles. Like I said, no accepting *anything* from anyone at the party. And if any one of us gets creeped out, we leave. No matter what. No matter if I'm feeling I'm onto something or whatever. We leave. We aren't being reckless."

She was almost pleading. I faced her, trying to look more concerned and caring than the scared I was feeling. "You'll be at a party where everyone is drinking and probably doing drugs as well, Madison. You never know what can happen at a party full of drunks."

There was no sound except the engine noise from the Beetle.

"I'll tell your dad." I sighed. "Only your dad, and it will be up to him to decide what to do from there."

More quiet.

Madison closed her eyes and sighed. "Okay. Yeah. Maybe his gift will show him we'll be okay and he won't freak. Mom would freak completely."

I released the brake and drove the few blocks to Cornelia House.

"I'll call him when I get to the hospital parking lot," I said as she unbuckled her seatbelt and opened her door.

She looked at me and nodded. "Yeah. I wish you wouldn't, but I can see why you have to. I, well, I haven't had any bad vibes about it all, but, yeah. Tell Papa and we'll see what happens."

She got out, gently shut the door behind her, and walked up the sidewalk to the house.

My heart ached as I watched her. Her Twombly giftedness might not be sending her any warnings, but my knowin' wasn't happy in the least. I put the Beetle in gear and pulled slowly away.

CHAPTER 13

BETTY THE CHARGE NURSE WAS AT THE NURSES' STATION.

"Hi, Betty. How is Jebbin doing? I hope he didn't give you too much trouble."

She smiled and chuckled. "No. No trouble at all, Mrs. Crawford. He was awake for about an hour. Then Dr. Christopoulos brought in a couple of big strappin' orderlies to help support your husband, seein' as he can't use his wrist yet for crutches, and they shuffled him over to the bathroom for a visit then back to his bed. Took a lot out of all of them I think, and your husband was lookin' pretty peaked when they tucked him back in. He's been sleepin' since then. Dr. C. said he was wantin' to get a feel for how ready Dr. Crawford is for goin' home and startin' his physical therapy. But he'll be tellin' you all about that when he does rounds early this evenin'."

"Sorry I missed the entertainment." I gave her a wink. "And thanks for letting me know Dr. Christopoulos will be coming by this evening. I'll make sure I'm here."

"You're welcome, Mrs. Crawford. I'll let Dr. C. know you'll be expectin' him to check in with you."

I turned to go to Jebbin's room then quickly turned back. "Oh, I almost forgot to tell you. Some friends of ours are going to stop by tonight. Dr. Nibodh Chatterjee, his wife Deepti, and their son. They'll know not to stay too long but they do want to see Jebbin."

Betty laughed. "Your forgettin' and rememberin' just reminded me. I was goin' to tell you that Mr. Twombly was here when they got your husband out of bed. He was wantin' to see how Dr. Crawford was doin' and he seemed excited about tellin' Dr. Christopoulos something. Any rate, he said there'd be some friends of yours coming to help with takin' care of Dr. Crawford when he goes home. Are these the same folks?"

"They are indeed, Betty."

She gave me a firm nod. "We do twelve hour shifts so I'll still be here. I'll also make sure my team knows to expect them and that they have clearance to be here even if it isn't proper visitin' hours."

"Thank you so much, Betty. You're a dear."

"Thank you. I became a nurse twenty-three years ago so I could be of help to folks, so it's my pleasure." She shooed me away with her hands. "You just go on and be with your husband, and if you need anythin' you just push the call button or come out here to the desk if you're wantin' to stretch."

"Will do," I said then headed down the hall to Jebbin's room.

Jebbin was asleep when I got to his room. I sat down on the not particularly comfortable plastic chair, which I'd pulled over near the phone for when the Chatterjees called. It was already 2:30 in the afternoon. I took out my Kindle and started to read the latest cozy mystery I was partway through.

 ⌁

"Mrs. Crawford. Mrs. Crawford!"

Betty was nudging my shoulder and calling my name.

"Hmm? What?" My feet had been put up on another chair that hadn't been there when I'd sat down, a pillow was behind my back and neck, a lightweight blanket was over me, and my Kindle had been shut off and set on the table by the telephone. The clock on the wall told me it was 5:15.

"The Chatterjees called earlier. They tried the room phone and no one answered, so they called the nurses' station. We let them know that you and Dr. Crawford were both nappin' and suggested they come up around five-thirty. I thought I'd come in and wake you so you can be ready when they get here. I put a wrapped toothbrush and toothpaste in the bathroom for you."

I pulled off my blanket, stiffly got my legs off the extra chair, stood up, and stretched. "I told you you're a dear, Betty," I said as I gave her a big hug. "Thanks."

She patted my back then broke the hug. "You're welcome, Hon," she said as she moved to the side of the bed. "I'll just be wakin' up Dr. Crawford and gettin' him tended to while you're busy."

The bedside phone rang as I walked out of the bathroom.

"Come on up any time, Chatty," Jebbin answered without even saying hello first. "Oh! Sorry, Jairus. We're expecting the Chatterjees any minute. By the way, thanks again for setting that up. It sure is going to make things a lot easier for Emory and me." He paused as Jairus spoke. "Yeah. She's right here."

Jebbin grinned as he held the portable handset out to me. "It's for you."

"Hello, Jairus."

"Hi, Emory. I'll try not to take long since Chatty and his family are due any minute. Just wanted to update you about Madison."

"I left a message ..."

"Yes. I didn't pick up because I was talking to Madison when you called. One of those times my intuition bothers her immensely,

I'm sure. I was in the foyer waiting for her to get home."

I smiled. "I should have expected it. I'm glad you were there."

"I let her present her case, then told her she could go, *but* I would be sending someone to keep an eye on her, Diane, and Doug. She started to explode, but I cut her off and told her it was someone who has often done security and surveillance work for the family and the college in the past, and she won't even know he's there.

"That mollified her a little. Madison knows that we have security at most of the functions we host and that the people always blend in. I asked her if she knew the age spread on these parties and type of people. She said she's been told that the age spread is everything from, I hate to say it, junior high kids to mid twenties or so. For the type of crowd, again it's a broad range from poor kids to rich, from kids everyone would think were too goody-goody to be there to ones that most people think are heading for jail."

Chatty and family knocked and Jebbin told them to come in. I smiled at them, held up a finger then pointed to the phone and ducked into the bathroom.

"The Chatterjees just came in and I'm in the bathroom," I explained to Jairus. "All I can say is, wow. These parties are bigger than I was expecting. I suppose the police know about them?"

"Yes, they know. But the parties are in a different place each time, or rotate between different locations from what I've been told by Sheriff Watkins. As far as law enforcement knows, they are always in old abandoned barns or heavy stands of trees with clearings in them and always outside of the city limits of any towns in Golden County. They're having a rough time getting anyone to admit to knowing anything about them. Madison said the plan she and the Daniels kids have is to find out at play practice either where the party is or find someone who will let Doug follow them. My people will be following Doug's car with a tracker so they won't all show up together. That might look suspicious. I'm actually going to have two people there. One will be watching the kids and one trying to sniff out information about how these things are set up and run. If we can find that out, we'll be a whole lot closer to figuring out who is behind it all."

"Sounds good," I said, even though I was still getting some niggling knowin' tingles down my back.

"No, it doesn't really," Jairus replied, and I reckoned whatever twitches or tingles he felt when his gift was trying to tell him something were acting up like mine were. "I'm scared about it all but have this very strong feeling that Madison needs to go, and that she'll be all right."

"I hope your gift is right. If you could, have your people keep an eye out for Melva. She as much as admitted that she goes to the parties."

"I hope my gift is right too. I'll let my people know about Melva and you'll know whatever I hear when I hear it."

"Same with me. Bye for now, Jairus."

"Later, Emory."

I breathed a prayer for Madison and the Daniels kids and went out to meet our friends.

＊

Deepti has told me that, no, she isn't an Indian princess—but to me she ought to be. Her name means *full of light*, or *to glow*—and she does. She moves with the bearing of a woman of self-confidence and strength that comes from her inner rule of kindness, and her deportment adds height to her five-foot stature. The men in her life rarely cross her out of a desire to please the woman who loves them so. And, other than Amy Twombly, she's the only woman I know well who could easily be a fashion model or a movie star. Deepti Chatterjee is simply a beautiful person.

"Emory!" she exclaimed as she rushed toward me, her long

dupatta scarf flowing out behind her. As we hugged the silk of her sky-blue *churidar kameez* outfit felt cool beneath my hands.

I've always loved the look of those South Asian leggings and tunic ensembles and the thought flitted through my mind that maybe, while she was here, Deepti and I could go shopping for a couple of them for me.

She pulled back to look at me. "We were so sorry to hear of Jebbin's accident, yet also pleased to hear that he is not hurt severely. We're so glad that it gives us an opportunity to be of help to you both." A broad smile lit her face. "Especially me. It is so unfair that Nibodh gets to come here so often, and I do not see the two of you nearly as much. I can hardly wait to be cooking for you, as you so often do for him."

Ragesh had followed behind his mother. "Hi, Auntie Emory. Can we go to your house soon? I wanna play with Sophie and start learning fiddle music." Ragesh's manner of speaking is much more American than his parents', but then, he was born and raised here so it should be. The boy was a delightful blend of his parents with skin that's not as dark as Chatty's nor as light as Deepti's. His face had his father's pleasant-though-average looks, softened by some of his mother's more graceful features. And, since, at ten years old he was already between the two of them in height, it was clear he would be taller than his father once he is done growing.

I looked at both of them. "I'm so glad you've come. Really. I was so worried about how I was going to handle helping Jebbin at home, dealing with all the housework, and doing everything else as well. And Jebbin gets so fussy when he can't have the lab covered when he has to be away for some reason." I looked at the boy. "We'll do some jamming, Ragesh. That is one of the best ways to turn violining into fiddling. I don't think Jebbin will be playing his banjo or guitar for a while because he hurt his left wrist, but he can still sing and we'll invite some of our bluegrass friends over to cover the other instruments. I think you'll be surprised how fast you'll catch on and how much fun it is."

We all gathered around Jebbin's bed for a couple of hours, sitting on extra chairs that the nurses found for us, conversation flowing between us all while Ragesh played games on his tablet or added his youthful observations to the discussion. But by 7:30, it was obvious that Jebbin was running out of steam. The Chatterjees and I went to Cracker Barrel for a late supper while Jebbin went back to sleep.

After our meal, I had the Chatterjees come with me back to our house. We talked some more on the screened porch then, around 10:30 as they were leaving, I gave them a key to the house and told them to come over whenever they wanted the next day.

"I know you have adjoining rooms at the hotel, but that's a hotel, not a home. Feel free to be here as much as you want," I told them.

Ragesh cheered. "Cool! What time do you feed Sophie and the cats in the morning? We brought my bike. I can ride over and take care of them all and then take Sophie for a walk." He winked at me. "You know, give Mom and Dad some alone time."

We all laughed at his youthful bluntness.

"That would be great, Ragesh. Between six and seven would be just fine. There's a new pet park on campus that you can take Sophie to. I'll leave a campus map on the kitchen table for you. She loves it there. I'll set the pet food and instructions about how much to give them on the table, too."

"Awesome! I'll be real careful with her, Auntie Emory. I won't let her run off. And I'll remember to lock the doors and take our keys with me when we're gone."

"Thank you, Ragesh. I'm sure you'll do just fine with it all."

After they left, I fed my fur-kids and put the pet food and map on the table for Ragesh. Then I just stood there by the kitchen table. The house felt so lonely without Jebbin there. Kumquat and Hortense jumped gracefully onto the table to give and get some loving while

Sophie lay down on my feet. They always know when their mom needs their affection. I loved them all up for about fifteen minutes, but I just couldn't stay home. I wanted to be at the hospital with Jebbin. So, after a few more hugs and cuddles, I packed a small travel bag with clean undies, toiletries, slippers, jammies, and a lightweight robe, then left. I'd just wear the same clothes tomorrow. My socks, jeans, and T-shirt were good for another day.

$$\approx$$

The nurses had already set up the portable bed for me. They'd figured me out quickly. At least this time I'd have my own toothbrush and my pajamas to sleep in. I changed, brushed my teeth, and sat for a while in the chair by Jebbin. He was still sleeping soundly, poor worn out man. The Chatterjees and I shouldn't have stayed until 7:30 talking to him. I sighed, took his right hand in mine, and kissed it. I gave the Lord another deep thank you for Jebbin not being hurt worse than he had been. After a few minutes of staring at my dear husband I picked up my Kindle.

Which I almost dropped when the bedside phone rang.

"At eleven-twenty at night?" I asked myself as I grabbed the receiver. "Hello?"

"Emory? Is that you?"

The voice was breathy.

Panicked.

Weepy.

"Madison?"

"Yes. Yes. Oh, Emory! It's awful! I'm so ... so ... I'm downstairs. I was ... was gonna go into the ER but they wouldn't let me in. I—we—Diane, Doug, and me. We ... didn't ... didn't see it. Heard it. Heard it while we were running for Doug's car. Guns. They had guns, Emory. Melva and Tom had guns. Tom ... Tom's dead. I ... felt it. I know he is. Stupid intuition gift thing—I know it. Can I come up? I need to come up."

I looked at Jebbin. He was out like a light. We wouldn't bother him.

"Yes. Come up as soon as you can. Melva Suter from the dig?" I stupidly asked. How many Melvas were there in Twombly? "Have you called your folks? Do they know?"

"Yeah. Melva Suter. I … I called … from the car. Asked Papa if I could come here. Asked Mama to come here, too. I want her, too." She snuffled hard. "These … they … they're people I know, Emory. People I know messin' with guns." She sniffed again. "Mama's here. Just walked in the door. We're coming up now."

The phone in my hand went quiet.

CHAPTER 14

IN A FEW MOMENTS THE TWOMBLY WOMEN WALKED IN THE DOOR OF Jebbin's hospital room, clinging together like contestants in a three-legged race.

Together they rushed to me and clutched me in. Madison was still overwrought—a crying, nose-dripping, snot-snuffling mess. Amy, though concerned and focused on her daughter, was amazingly in control of herself. She radiated caring emotions while not being overly emotional herself and adding to Madison's state. But then, Amy looked up and I saw her eyes. She was terrified. I could sense the thoughts in her mind as they raced by. *"Maddy could have been hurt! A shot might have gone wild! Why did we let her go? Where did the kids get the pistols? How much did Maddy see? Oh my God! A boy was killed!"*

And more that was inexpressible.

How did I know all this? Perhaps it was my gifted knowin's.

No. I'm a mom too, and I was feeling it all myself.

"They started arguing." Madison's low voice broke the moment. "Melva and ... Tom. We ... we were there when they started arguing."

Madison took a few breaths. Amy and I said nothing.

"They must have been at it for a bit. Someone had turned the music way down and we ... um. Suddenly we could all hear them arguing. Gambling. They ... they were arguing about gambling. Tom was ranting that Melva owed him ... and ... and she was cussing a blue streak at him, saying she didn't owe *him* anything." Madison started crying hard again.

Amy hugged her and sighed. "There seems to be—well. You've most likely read about it in the *Golden County Gazette*. It appears there's a problem with illegal gambling in the county and a lot of kids from the high school and Twombly College might be involved as well as adults. Law enforcement has been going nuts trying to get a fix on it, but haven't so far."

Madison nodded and went on. "Yeah. I've a feeling it's part of all that. Someone, not ... not sure who ..." She took three long deep breaths, struggling to stop crying, so she could get the story told. "Someone yelled 'Duel! Duel! Duel!' and others took it up and ... it was like a play. It was like ... totally out of nowhere, Tom and Melva had pistols ... and ... and." She breathed some more. "Did the whole standing back-to-back thing and pacing off."

Madison looked at her mom and me, then worked free of the huddle we were in and sat down on the plastic chair. Amy and I sat on the portable bed across from her.

Madison went on. "Diane, Doug, and I—we all thought they, Melva and Tom, had set this all up. You know, like they were ... were just acting it out. We figured the guns were fake and ... they were just goofing around. Most everyone else thought the same thing. It was funny."

She shut her eyes. Pain and frustration at the memory pinched her face.

"Yeah. Funny," she huffed, opened her eyes, and went on. "They could hardly stand up, let alone … let alone walk, but they, ah … they tottered the ten steps. I think most people were too drunk to … to, you know, notice and think it through. I mean … it was like no one backed away."

Her eyes went wide as she realized how that sounded.

"We did," she said in a panic, afraid her Mom and I would think they'd been that stupid. "Diane, Doug, and I. We moved back quite a ways, and so did some other kids who must've not been drinking and could still think straight. We all, you know, were just unsure enough that we … yeah. We moved back. Melva and Tom … started to turn when …" She swallowed. "Melva's gun went off. She was pointing it down instead of up and … and it kicked up a bunch of dirt. It got really quiet for … well, probably one of those things when it seemed like, you know, like forever but … but it was only a couple of seconds. Everybody knew the guns were loaded after that. Then some of the people that were drunk the worst … they, ah, started laughing and cheering, and some that weren't as far gone started screaming and backing off but still watching. And you suddenly knew who was the most sober 'cause we were all scared, pulling out cellphones, and running away."

She stopped.

Just stopped.

Suddenly dry-eyed.

She swiped at her nose with the sleeve of her lightweight jacket then lay her hands on her thighs where they started rubbing and picking at her jeans. She looked at her mom and me.

"No. I … um, I lied to you guys. When I called home, Mama, ah … and when I called you, Emory, um … after the Daniels' dropped me off here at the hospital." Madison closed her eyes and drew herself up to sit very stiff and straight. "I saw it happen. I saw it all."

Her eyes slowly opened to stare blindly at a blank wall across from her. Her eyes weren't seeing, but her mind was running a replay of a murder.

"I ran with Diane and Doug a few steps, but then I turned and watched. I wasn't real close, but it was weird. There was a gap, you know, an open space in the crowd of people who hadn't run away. So weird. This … this perfect hole between Melva and Tom and me. Like it was a play on a stage and the side toward the audience had to be open so they could see … and I was the audience. I couldn't see details but I could see how Tom and Melva moved and could hear some of what they were saying. They were both swaying. Tom was laughing and pointing at her because Melva'd shot the ground. Melva was staring at the hole in the ground and kept repeating the f'ing gun was loaded. I think she was stunned or scared or … something."

Madison blinked a couple of slow blinks, grimaced, and went on.

"Tom yelled 'My turn!' pointed his gun at her, and shot. It … um … I think it nicked her leg 'cause she yelled—something like *ow* or *ouch*, and grabbed at the outside of her thigh. Then Melva said *damn*. She looked at Tom. Swore at him … Swore at him and swung the gun up as she swore and started shaking it like she was shaking her finger at him like he was a naughty kid. The gun … No. Can't blame the gun, though Melva may not have even realized that she was pulling the trigger because she kept right on shaking the gun and cussing at Tom the whole time. Like all she really cared about was cussing Tom out. There was a blast. Tom … stumbled back and crumpled to the ground. Then this Goth guy grabbed me. He ran carrying me to Doug's car, shoved me in, banged on the roof and yelled at Doug to get out of there. So we barreled outta there like he told us to."

She looked at her mom and me again.

"I think the Goth guy was Papa's security guy."

After a pause I'd finally thought to ask her what had happened to Melva.

"I don't know," she sighed. "Last I saw her, Melva was standing there staring at the gun in her hand as though she'd never seen a pistol or a hand before. Just standing there while everyone else scattered everywhere."

The three of us sat together in silence until her mother and I heard Madison softly snoring and Amy said she should get her exhausted daughter home. Mother and daughter left as they'd come, holding onto each other, and I tucked myself into my portable bed.

CHAPTER 15

I WOKE TO THE RUMBLE OF THUNDER. DOOOOM. GLOOOOM.
It grumbled, suiting my mood just fine.

The time on my cellphone was 6:45. The weather on my cellphone
said scattered thunderstorms throughout the day, some with heavy
rain but none severe, and it seemed it was right.

I didn't want to move. I was still wrung out from yesterday and
especially last night.

Doom and Gloom.

With another drumroll of thunder, I decided it was time to be
up, so to speak. I didn't rise and shine, but at least I sat up in my
bed, turned on the TV, turned down the volume so as not to wake
Jebbin, and found the station that shows local programing. The
morning edition of the news from Golden County was on.

Yep. The TV weather agreed with my cellphone weather.

The newscaster took five minutes to read off, and discuss, the
rankings for the various summer bowling league teams and another

five to report on the children's and adult's softball leagues.

But then …

"Our top story this morning is the shooting death of Illinois State University sophomore Tom Knox, of Chicago, at one of the drinking and drug parties that have been eluding law enforcement officials in Golden County all spring and summer. Wounded in the altercation was Twombly High School junior Melva Suter, of Twombly. Ms. Suter was treated at Memorial Hospital of Twombly and released into the custody of the Golden County Sheriff's Department. She is being held at the county jail pending further investigation. Several others at the party, many of them minors, were also taken into custody at the scene and are either being held at the jail or have been released temporarily into the custody of their parents or guardians. Repeating, our top story this morning is the shooting death of an Illinois State University sophomore and the wounding of a Twombly High School junior at a drinking and drug party in rural Golden County last night."

I shut the sad news off.

"Well," I muttered to myself as I got up onto my feet to go use the bathroom, "guess I know where Melva is this morning."

My cell's text message tone sounded while I was in the middle of brushing my teeth, so I hurried the process and popped out to check it. It was from Ceek.

Got texts from a few of our team who were at THE party last night or are family or friends of ones who were. I've decided we're taking today off. See you all Monday.

Normally we worked a half-day on Saturday and only had Sunday as a full day off but I was sure this was a good decision. If some of the team had been at the party they were most likely hung over anyway, or, if they had family and friends who had been there, they might be dealing with having a loved one in jail, even if only temporarily.

"Mornin'."

I smiled and looked over at my good man in his hospital bed.

"Mornin', Hon! How're you this morning?"

Jebbin stretched his arms up, even the left one with its lightweight cast.

"I'm doing much better." He reached out and pulled me over. I sat on the edge of his bed, putting aside my dreary mood as we shared a good morning kiss and cuddle. I didn't want to ruin his obvious good mood.

"Time to call a nurse in," Jebbin eventually said, reaching up for his call button. "I want to keep the flooding outside." He winked at me. I stood and headed back to the bathroom to finish my own morning routine.

I came out as nurse Joan was taking Jebbin's vitals.

"Good morning, Mrs. Crawford." She was much younger than nurse Betty, in her early twenties I would say, and as perky as a sunny day. "I just told Dr. Crawford that Dr. Christopoulos is already on the floor this morning and should be in here in about half an hour. You may want to wait before you go to breakfast."

"Yes, thank you, Joan. I don't want to miss him. Is there somewhere other than the cafeteria where I can get some coffee? That should hold me over till I can get breakfast."

"You can go to the second floor lobby. There's a small coffee bar there. No seating or anything, just a showcase with pastries and goodies and really good coffee, tea, and juices." She beamed.

"That'll be perfect. Thanks. Can I bring you anything, Jebbin?" I asked as I grabbed my purse and headed for the door.

"Oh yeah! I'm sure I'll regret it later when I need to pee more, but a large coffee and a couple of pastries you know I'll like."

Off I went in search of the coffee bar. I was wondering how to broach the topic of the death at the party to Jebbin. Right now, he needed to focus on learning his physical therapy exercises, how to handle a wheelchair, and how much of his day-to-day needs he should, would, could be doing for himself—not worrying about a case that he most likely wouldn't be able to work on but would have been working on if he hadn't fallen into a sunken house. I got Jebbin his large black coffee and a mega cinnamon roll, and a large hazelnut latte and moderate-sized cinnamon roll for myself. As I went back to his room I thought over how I'd break the news about Tom Knox's death to him after we saw Dr. Christopoulos.

"Did you know there was a murder last night?" was the first thing out of Jebbin's mouth when I walked in his door.

"Um … Yeah. Yeah, I knew. I saw it on the local news this morning." I reckoned he didn't need to know, yet, that I was much more involved than merely watching it on the news, that I had an eyewitness report last night. "How did you find out?"

"Joan the nurse told me right after you left to get the coffee and pastries. I'm going to need to be at the lab." He looked at his arm and leg in their casts. "How can I be at the lab like this?" he sulked.

By now I was at his bedside placing the cup caddy and bag from the coffee bar on his tray. "We don't know much about what you can or can't do yet, and you know Chatty and his family came here, in part, just so there would be someone to handle the lab if something came up."

"Yeah," was his petulant reply, but then his eyes lit up as I pulled the huge cinnamon roll, paper plate and all wrapped in plastic wrap, out of the bag. "If this is a peace offering, it's a good one. Good Lord, that looks scrumptious!"

"And a large black coffee to go with it." I grinned as I removed the plastic cover from his cup. "I know you're disappointed, Hon, but who knows? There may be more you can do than we think. We'll just have to see what Dr. Christopoulos has to say."

"You shouldn't be eating that humongous roll, is what he has to say."

Jebbin and I jumped a bit and turned toward the door where

Dr. Christopoulos stood chuckling.

"Yep. I *have* to say that as your doctor, but I will add that I fall victim to their siren's song once a month every month. I too am a mere mortal, which is hard to get any surgeon to admit."

We all laughed.

"If they're that good," Jebbin grinned as I started to remove the wrapping, "don't expect me to offer to share."

Dr. Christopoulos laughed again, holding his hands up in surrender. "Oh no. I wouldn't ever expect that. I never share mine either." He flipped open his notes. "You go ahead and eat while I give you all the latest news on this Jebbin Crawford guy. Let's see. They've been having you sit up in bed, so you've been approved for spending most of your time upright." He glanced at Jebbin. "As long as your leg is at least parallel to the floor or a bit higher. Having said that, in a moment I'm expecting someone to show up with a wheelchair so you can go for a ride around the floor up here."

"Goo noo." My hubby mumbled around a mouthful of cinnamon roll.

"Yes. Good news indeed." Dr. Christopoulos was good at translating. "And then, your friend and ours here at Memorial of Twombly, Jairus Twombly, researched some alternatives to wheelchairs and crutches. He then presented his findings to me, the orthopedic staff, and the physical therapy staff, and we've selected an appliance that we feel will work very well for you." He paused and blushed. "I, ah, am hesitant to say that we hadn't heard of it. Between a bunch of orthopods and physical therapists we're supposed to keep up on all the little goodies that come out. But we missed this one. Glad Jairus found it though and you get to be the guinea pig."

I brightened up at this. "You mean I might not have to fight with hauling my tiny husband in and out of a wheelchair?"

The doctor and I both looked at my slightly chubby, big-boned, six-foot-tall husband.

"Well, that's part of why we're glad to have Jebbin as our trial subject. If this works well with a big husky person, we'll know it's stable, sturdily built, and will be able to handle bigger-sized patients. Then, when we get a smaller-built patient we'll test it on them to be sure it's not too heavy for them to use. If it clears both ends of the spectrum, we know we have a new aid for most any patient who can't use crutches. With Jebbin, we're hoping this will totally replace his needing a chair fairly early on, but I'm acquisitioning a chair for you anyway. It's always good to have one readily available to fall back on if needed."

"Don't say 'fall back on,' Doctor," Jebbin chided. "I've had more than enough fallin' in any direction to last me a good while."

"Good point. Let's just say readily available if needed. Better?"

"Much."

We shared another round of laughter.

"It's called The Walk About and we expect it to arrive sometime this morning," Dr. Christopoulos went on. "We're going to have a couple of the PTs test it out after it's assembled, but of course it won't be exactly the same as having a person with injuries on it. That's why Jebbin is the important guinea pig. We will want you here, Emory, when we're ready to put it on Jebbin's leg. You will need to know how to secure it properly and to understand how to be a spotter for him until he's completely comfortable and confident on it."

"Yes, of course. And I'll let our friends the Chatterjees know to be ready for a call when it comes. They have come to Twombly to help us out while Jebbin's leg is healing, so they—well, especially Mrs. Chatterjee—will need to know about it too."

"Then, yes, she needs to be here too. We want everyone who might help care for Jebbin to be here to see how this works and learn how to properly position his lower leg on it. We'll have everyone," he looked over at his patient, "including you, Jebbin, learn how to take it on and off. It has been designed so that people can take it on and off themselves."

He paused. "And then, even bigger news. If you do well with being in the wheelchair and if you take well to The Walk About, Jebbin, you will be going home sometime this afternoon."

Cheers erupted and we were surprised no one came to tell us to quiet down.

⁂

After Dr. Christopoulos left, and Jebbin and I had a nice time wondering what the Walk About gizmo was going to be like, all the coffee he'd drunk made a visit from a nurse necessary. I took the handset from Jebbin's room phone and went out in the hall to call Deepti Chatterjee, deciding ahead that if she didn't pick up after the second ring I'd try later—in case she and Chatty were having some alone time at the hotel.

She picked up right away.

"Ah, yes, Ragesh and his kindly mentioning to you his wish to give his parents the gift of some alone time," she responded when I enquired why she had answered so quickly, then laughed her merry melodic laugh. "Alas, if you did not know, there was a murder last night and my ever dutiful husband left for the lab around five o'clock this morning. He hopes he will have the ballistics done before anything else from the shooting comes in. He is also most eager to help answer the questions that have arisen over the mummies from the house Jebbin fell into."

I nodded, though she couldn't see it. "Yes. I knew. I just wasn't sure if you all did. I should have figured you did seeing as Jairus arranged for you to come, in part, so the lab would be covered. I'd been so focused on the sunken house and the mummies that I'd forgotten he'd be doing work on the shooting case first."

"Yes, murder in the present comes before murder in the past. Also you should know that, to Ragesh's great disappointment, I drove him to your house today and that is where I am now. I think he had been looking forward to his own alone time here this morning, but he will have to be patient and have that another time."

The strange phrase she used caught at my mind, as though I needed to remember it. Murder in the present comes before murder in the past. I knew how she meant it, but it seemed … strange. For right now I had to tuck it aside.

"Did you drive up in two cars or did you both get up with Chatty this morning?" I asked.

"No." She laughed again. "We did all come in the same car yesterday, but we brought all our bicycles. I with the thunderstorm going on, I drove Ragesh to your house when he was ready to come take care of dear Sophie and the kitties. Nibodh, being the good husband and father that he is, rode his bike to the lab earlier so we could have the protection of the car."

"Very sensible. I called to let you all know that there is a very good chance that Jebbin will be coming home later today …"

"Wonderful!" Deepti cut me off.

"Yes, it is great news. Even better, Jairus, Jebbin's doctor, and the physical therapy staff have come up with some product they've purchased that is supposed to allow Jebbin to get around without a wheelchair or crutches. They want you to come when it arrives, sometime this morning, when they see if it will work as expected and if Jebbin gets the hang of it well enough. You and I, as his caregivers, need to be here so we can learn how to put it on and take it off his leg correctly."

"Wonderful!" she exclaimed again. "It will be a true blessing if he can be free of a wheelchair. May Ragesh come as well? I'm certain he will find the aid fascinating and perhaps he should also learn how to attach and remove it. It would not hurt to have another of us be able to do so."

"Great idea, Deepti. Yes, bring Ragesh. They are not sure when it ... oh, it's called The Walk About ... they don't know when it will get here and I'm sure they want some time to look it over first before they bring it in to try on Jebbin. I'll need to call you whenever I get word it's all about to happen. Can you and Ragesh stay available?"

"No problem, Emory. Ragesh is presently at the Pet Park with Sophie but when he is back we will do something with our time that is easy to stop at a moment's notice. No problem at all." There was a slight pause. "I just thought, this means that Jebbin and you both are likely to be home for dinner tonight, does it not?"

"Oh my! Good thinking, Deepti. Yes, it does. I'm so glad you thought of it. I would have felt bad to have caught you off guard later in the day."

"Again, my friend, no problem. I will prepare something that simmers most of the day, makes a lot, and is good the next day as well, so it will work no matter what happens."

"Perfect. I should go. I'll call you when they're ready to try out The Walk About."

"My phone will be with me. We will see you then."

My mind was buzzing now with the strange way Deepti had expressed that a current murder with a real-time victim and killer took precedence over a crime that happened over one hundred and fifty years in the past.

And I knew where I needed to go to get my head clear.

"Hon?" I addressed Jebbin as I walked back into his room.

"Yep." He was so cheery I hated to ask if I could leave for a bit.

"Would you mind too much if I run over to Mysterious Ways? I know I'm out of that chai Aine makes that the Chatterjees like so much and I'd like to pick some up so we have it available, since they're going to be here for a while."

He smiled. "Don't mind at all, Darlin'. Get some of that blackberry sage tea from that one commercial company she carries while you're there."

"Yes, *The Republic of Tea* is the brand. I will," I said as I grabbed my purse, went over, kissed him, and headed out the door to see Aine.

CHAPTER 16

AINE MCALLISTER WAS ONE OF MY BEST FRIENDS AND THE PROPRIETRESS
of Mysterious Ways: Plants, Herbs & Irish Blessings. Both the shop
and its owner had a mystical feel to them and I often went there
when seeking insight into problems I deal with.

"I was wondering when you'd be in here." Aine's voice came from
somewhere at the back of the shop as I stepped over the threshold.

"Having visions of me, were you?"

"No," she said in a softer volume as she appeared from the room
where she did all her work arranging fresh cut and dried flowers.
"Jebbin's been hurt and is in hospital …"

"Speaking of that," I interrupted her, "thank you so much for
the lovely arrangement you sent."

"You're welcome." She smiled her big, beautiful smile. "I made
it full of things that bring healing and encouragement. Where was
I? Oh, yes! Jebbin in hospital, the mysterious Sutton House found
by said husband falling into it, and now there's been a murder at

one of this summer's nefarious wild parties. Of course, my friend Emory will be coming in."

She paused, looking at me with that look only she can get, like she's looking within and beyond you. "Your aura is very mixed today. You're tired, excited, eager, and befuddled all at the same time." She went over to the teas section of the shop. "I know what you're needing." She paused again. "Two of my helping blends and a large container of my India Glory Chai."

"Okay, how did you know about the chai?"

She turned and gave me a Cheshire Cat grin while batting her lashes at me. "How do you know some of the things you know?"

I laughed. "Point taken."

"If Dr. Crawford might be out of commission, Dr. Chatterjee might be coming to Twombly. Since you will probably need help at home with a big, tall man with one leg and one wrist in casts, and it's summer, then there is a possibility that Dr. Chatterjee may bring his wife and son along with him."

"The longer I know you the less mystical you are and the more Holmesian you become."

"You've said that before, Emory, but it's still elementary, my dear Miss Marple."

We chuckled over the references.

"Though you missed the blackberry sage tea Jebbin asked for."

"He isn't here for me to get his vibes, is he?" She plopped a tin of teabags of the commercially made tea on the counter, winked at me, then turned back to the shelves of her own blends. "The teas *you* need are Realignment and Discernment, one to fix your poor aura and the other to fix your poor overloaded thinking."

"I have had a lot to deal with the last few days and we both know I can't focus on too many things at a time."

"And there's more coming your way." She didn't explain that but turned from getting the required teas from her shelves and started putting my order into one of the shop's Mysterious Ways are the Best Ways bags, which are made from recycled paper and completely biodegradable. Aine wouldn't have any other kinds of bags. "Drink some Discernment tea as soon as you can. It will work on its own to help free your subconscious to work on your questions. Realignment will be best drunk when you have time available for quietness and solitude."

I swiped my debit card while wondering when was I going to find time for either with Deepti, Ragesh, and Jebbin all in my house everyday and me busy with old and new mysteries for the foreseeable future.

Aine picked up one of her business cards and began to write something on the back of it.

"I recommend either the Japanese Garden or the J.M. Ramm Musical Garden. Realignment likes the vibes in those gardens. Also, you need to let Discernment play with your thoughts. Don't try to guide it too much."

She handed me the card.

The familiar tingling crept up my back, causing a short, swift shiver as I grasped the card.

"I … ah, okay, Aine. I … um, need to go. Told Jebbin I wouldn't be long."

I left the shop and stopped at the corner before going on to the car. On the back of the card Aine had printed in Irish Gaelic, in her tiny precise hand:

Uaireanta ní bheidh an am atá caite fanacht san am atá caite.

And below it: *Sometimes the past won't stay in the past.*

CHAPTER 17

I WANTED TO THINK ABOUT IT ALL.

Aine's message on her business card and Deepti's off-hand comment. I knew, I just plain *knew*, they were both important. But, I didn't have the time to think about it now; I needed to get back to Jebbin.

It was about 10:30 when I got back to his room … and found he was gone.

Not dead gone, thank the Lord, but just not in the room. A quick stop at the nurses' station sent me to the lobby/solarium on his floor where my dear man was in a wheelchair parked by the floor to ceiling windows.

"Not the cheeriest view, all the grey skies and more rain falling, but at least in here I can see more than just the clouds."

He spoke before I got to him.

"You heard me coming?" I asked as I crossed the carpeted part of the room.

Jebbin laughed, reaching for me with his uninjured right hand as he did. "Nah. I saw your reflection in the window."

He gave my hand a squeeze and I bent to give his lips a kiss.

"I get to go home today." He sighed pleasurably when our kiss ended.

"Indeed you do." I kissed the top of his head this time before turning to find a chair to pull over so I could sit next to him. "And, if you're a good boy and do as you're told," I sat in the chair I found, "maybe you can go to the lab and be of some help to Chatty in a few days. That is if The Walk About thingy works well for you."

He harrumphed. "I'll be at the lab tomorrow even if it's in the wheelchair. You know there's an elevator in the building and most of the tables in there are open underneath. Plenty of room to have my elevated leg under one of them."

"True. Very true." I looked out the window at the hospital's garden that was set into the open space of the U-shaped building. "Rain's pretty light now," I observed. "Other than the ground saturation, I don't think more rain will hurt the dig any. The levee is still broken through, and I think any more flooding will just drain into Rock Lake. Then it will flood to the south, away from the dig site."

"Now that you mention it," Jebbin turned to look at me, "why are you here? Shouldn't you be at the site?"

"Oh! I'm sorry, Hon. I forgot to tell you, with everything else going on, that Ceek cancelled for today. We start up again on Monday. There were ... well, some of the team are either family or friends to kids that were at that party last night. And Ceek said some of the students on the team might've even have been there themselves. Some had texted him asking off, so he decided to just call the morning's dig time off."

"Hmm. I can see that." He wearily shook his head. "What a sad, sad mess. Have you heard any more about it?"

It only took me a few seconds to decide to tell my good man

about Madison's account from last night. Jebbin has always been my trusted confidant. He is as good at keeping a confidence as was my father, the Methodist pastor. And, I reckoned that since he already knew about the shooting, not telling him was rather moot.

So I told him.

"Wow!" He said when I was completely finished. "She's havin' some odd life experiences for a rich family's kid. This makes the second murdered body she's seen and this time she saw the murder happenin'." His accent was more pronounced, showing how deeply he was feeling for Madison. "And Melva! Goodness, what a mess for her and Larry."

"Yes." I let my eyes wander to the window and the weeping world outside. "I feel so badly for both of them. Melva's been doing so well on the dig. You know, she did every job she was given with no complaints and did it with thoroughness as well. And Larry works so hard to keep his restaurant in the black." I looked over at Jebbin. "It always gets a good-star rating and I've never seen it written up in the paper for having problems with health inspections."

"Yep, and that takes a lot of effort and keepin' a close eye on the staff."

"Deepti told me … oh! I called her this morning so she knows to expect a call when they're ready to try The Walk About on you. But as I was saying, Deepti told me that Chatty went over to the lab early this morning. They were called about the shooting, so he knew evidence would be coming in. They have both of the guns from the duel and he'll be running ballistics on them. I'm so hoping that somehow she didn't shoot the boy."

"No intuition about it?" Though the subject was most serious, Jebbin grinned as he usually did whenever he asked about my gift.

"No. Not really. It seems to be busy with other things today. But the way Madison said Melva was shaking the gun at Tom. Like an angry person shaking their finger in someone's face. Just seems strange that a shot from a gun that's moving that much would find a fatal target." I shrugged. "But I'm sure weirder things than that have happened with guns before."

"You're right there." He nodded. "That's why ballistics and the other tests we run are so important. Blood spatter. Fibers. Plant matter. All too often, that stuff tells us that a crime wasn't done in the manner that seems to be so obvious. Who knows, though, you might be right."

"Dr. Crawford?" Came a voice from a distance. We both turned to see nurse Joan in the lobby that fed into the hall with the patient rooms.

"The Walk About arrived and the doctors and PTs have had the time to assemble it and play with it. They'll be up in a few minutes to test it out on you."

I released the brake, grabbed the handles on Jebbin's wheelchair, and jogged him down the hall to his room, calling Deepti on the room phone as soon as I had him parked and put the chair's brake back on.

"Okay, Jebbin." Dr. Salim said. "Now, I want your foot and the 'leg' on the unit about a shoulder width apart, then let me and Tony do all the lifting like before and we'll get you standing up again."

We were on adjustment number four. "We" meaning Jebbin, me, the doctors and physical therapy folks, Deepti, Ragesh, and Jairus. I'm sure there would have been more curious medical personnel interested in seeing the new appliance tested out, but the room was crowded as it was.

I have to admit that to me it looked impossible to use the thing while moving comfortably or with good balance. But Tony had strapped it on, walked around Jebbin's room and up and down the hallway, looking for all the world like he had been wearing the thing his whole life. And he'd only tried it a few times before they brought it upstairs.

When it was finally adjusted properly, they had Jebbin stand. Just stand. First holding onto Tony and then on his own. Next came doing some stretches while standing to get his body used to balancing, and finally, the big moment of taking a step. Amazingly, after only a dozen or so slow halting steps, Jebbin was walking. Then they showed him how to sit down properly with the unit on as well.

After all that, we could tell Jebbin was getting worn out and soon he was back in bed.

"We'll send you home today, Jebbin," Dr. Christopoulos announced, grinning from ear to ear. "We're sending Tony with you. He is also a home health provider so he can help with personal care that might be too difficult for Emory and Deepti to handle. He'll be doing your PT with you and will keep us advised on how you're progressing."

Release time was set for three in the afternoon. Tony would be staying at our house in the guest room on the main level, the room that used to be our son Lanthan's bedroom. Jebbin would be sleeping in our room right next door with an intercom, in case he needed Tony's help during the night.

And so, after a few more congratulations, everyone left, Jebbin fell asleep, and I headed for the cafeteria for a late lunch …

… and a phone call to Madison.

CHAPTER 18

I BREATHED OUT A SIGH AS I SET DOWN MY TRAY AND PLOPPED INTO my chair. Not sure what type of sigh … Relief? Satisfaction? Release of tension? All of the above was the option I went with. As much as it was going to be strange having Tony full time at the house, I was greatly relieved that someone would be there overnight. And, if I understood aright, everyone was pretty confident that we wouldn't need in-home help for long.

So far, so good.

Release of tension? It had been a strange morning so far. Busy and anxious. It felt good to be alone with my thoughts and a good lunch.

Satisfaction? Well. Things with Jebbin and the cases were … hmm, sort of moving along.

I took a big bite of my BLT, which was made fresh to order like many of the sandwiches here were, and sighed another sigh. This one was definitely satisfaction. Firm whole grain bread, just the right amount of mayo, crispy bacon, and crispy lettuce, flavorful

Roma tomatoes that were never too drippy. I couldn't have made it better myself.

My phone rang.

I had turned it on in anticipation of calling Madison.

Who was now calling me.

"Hi, Madison." I greeted her.

"Hi, Emory. I took a chance that you were having some lunch now. Are you alone? Can you talk?"

"Took a chance or knew I'd be available?" I said and chuckled.

"Knew, of course."

We both laughed, though the young teen's laugh seemed a bit strained.

"I heard from Papa that everything's lookin' good with Dr. Crawford. He said the no-crutch walking thingy was really cool and worked really well. I'm happy for you both. Everything will be a lot easier when you don't have to be at the hospital anymore."

"That's for sure! If nothing else, it will be soooo nice to sleep in my own bed."

"I know that feeling," she agreed. "I've got some news for you. Not tons, but I think it's good stuff."

"Go for it," I encouraged her. I had almost said "shoot" but, having heard the strain in her voice, thought better of it. Not a good choice of words after all Madison had been through last night.

"Papa called Melva's dad last night to offer Mrs. Bogardus' assistance. I think he tried to say no, but Papa said he knew Mr. Suter had a business lawyer but this would need someone with experience in criminal law."

"You know this how?" I interrupted.

"Ah …" I could sense the microprocessors humming away in her little grey cells. "You know I have my ways, and … um, this is an old house with all sorts of nooks and crannies that people have forgotten about over the years."

"You snooped?"

I could picture the tilt of her head and proud look in her eyes as she told me, "No. I gathered intelligence."

I looked heavenward in resignation. What could I say? I wanted the information. "Go on."

"So anyway, Papa said that since he knew they would be questioning Melva really soon, Mrs. Bogardus, who handled things for Mama last January, could sit in on the sessions as their temporary counsel until he found a suitable criminal lawyer. Melva's dad agreed and so that's what happened."

My mind was taking in her words, but was still troubled about their source. "You were here late last night and early this morning," I reminded her. "How did you ... Never mind. What I don't know I don't have to try to hide when they arrest you for some sort of electronic eavesdropping."

Her laugh sounded less strained this time. "Good choice. Anyway, about ten or so this morning, Mrs. Bogardus came to the house to talk to Papa about the questioning at the police station. I took notes."

I had a flash image of Madison crouching in some dusty priest's hole type space with her pencil and stenographer's pad, and was amazed all over again that a modern-day fifteen-year-old could still be fluent with Gregg's Shorthand.

"Um, the officer started with the argument between Melva and Tom. Melva admitted that she gambles and that she owed Tom a couple hundred bucks. Police asked if that was all there was to the argument, just the gambling debt. She said yeah, she thought it was but she was pretty drunk and her memory of stuff at that point wasn't very good. The officer pressed about the gambling. Melva said there're games all over Golden County. Nothing big, she said. All sorts of people and all kinds of ages, even junior high kids who come with older siblings or friends who can drive."

"Hmm ..." I muttered. "Just like the descriptions of the crowds at the parties."

"Yeah." I could picture her nodding. "Yeah, exactly. It really was like that last ..."

It was a noticeable pause and her voice was weak when she spoke. "It was like that last night. There were really young kids there watching ... it."

I knew which "it" she meant.

"Ah, anyway," Madison continued. "She said Tom had started following her around at the party last night, bugging her non-stop about paying him back. One thing that caught my attention was that, according to Melva, Tom said he knew just who to go to if he needed muscle to get the money from her, and that she knew who he meant."

"Did she know?"

"Mrs. Bogardus thought so. Said Melva got flushed at that question. Then the officer asked if Melva knew someone named Peter Westford. Melva said she did. Mrs. Bogardus said that was not surprising since he distributes all the gambling machines in Golden and Sullivan counties and there are machines at The Coal Bin. Then Mrs. B. said that the officer went straight from that to who came up with the idea of dueling over the debt between Melva and Tom. Melva said she didn't know. More than one person, she thought, just started saying they should have a duel. Then it turned into a chant that made her head ache, and all of a sudden she had a gun in her hand.

"I'll put in here that that's what I saw and heard. I heard them arguing but didn't really pay attention 'cause it wasn't the first argument that popped up. But then people were laughing and chanting 'duel' and, like I told you and Mama last night, Diane, Doug, and I started paying attention then. You know, when the word duel got included. And the crowd didn't clear so that I could see them until they ... well, until they actually did the back-to-back and pacing off thing, so I didn't have a chance to see how they got the guns."

We were quiet after that, each with our own thoughts.

"Well," Madison softly said. "Um. After that, Mrs. B. said that the cop, who apparently was being pretty gentle with Melva, re-asked a couple of things. She started crying and saying she really wished she did know who the person was. Said it was their fault as much as hers and Tom's that it all happened 'cause it couldn't have happened if there hadn't been guns there. Mrs. Bogardus said the cop changed the subject to what he said other kids were calling the 'high octane' booze. And that's when the whole feeling to her report to Papa changed."

"How so?"

"Her voice got softer, and she said now she was getting to something that truly worried her. She said Melva got all closed in when the booze got mentioned. Oh! I need to back up a bit. I totally forgot about this when I told you about everything last night. There was this weird detail to the party. We—Diane, Doug, and I, were told to bring twenty bucks with us. No one would explain, we were just told we had to have it. So we got there and there was only one way into the place. No one parked at the entrance. The car we followed pulled into a cornfield on an access lane, then into a small bare spot in the field. We were maybe half a block away, but you wouldn't have spotted the cars from the main roads. Everyone went up to the gate and paid the big thug type guys there the twenty bucks to get in."

"Like a cover charge at a bar." I nodded.

"Yeah," she quickly confirmed. "Not that I've ever been at a place like that, but I've seen it on TV shows and movies. But I got one of my feelings that this was a way to say they weren't selling any of the alcohol to kids. You paid to get in. Once in, the snacks and drinks were free. And they had sodas and fruit drinks and bottled water available, not just beer and hard stuff. And it was all help yourself. I think that way they could say they didn't even serve it to minors.

It was just there."

"Sounds about right," I said. "Clever, but I don't think it would stand up in court. Hard to say."

"Yeah. I think you're right. Anyway, Mrs. Bogardus went on that Melva really clammed up when the officer asked about the strong booze. You know, one-word answers and that sort of thing. She said she could tell the officer picked up on it, too, and told her they were going to be finding out all about it. That they'd had plenty of the kids they were holding who had thrown up in the cells, and … Mrs. B. said this really hit Melva hard … that they'd be analyzing Tom's stomach contents, and they'd know what the stuff was before the end of the day today.

"Mrs. Bogardus also said it was the only time that Mr. Suter reacted much. She said she'd heard a gasp or something from him, and that he started in asking Melva questions about it. Saying that she'd been brought up in a restaurant with a bar and that she knew about different kinds of booze and didn't she have some kind of idea what it was."

"He had a good point."

"Yeah. I thought so too. And that was kinda the end of things. Mrs. Bogardus said that Melva swore that she'd only seen and drunk regular booze like you buy at the store. They asked her about drugs and she said there was stuff there but she'd only drunk the booze. She said she's had some bad experiences with drugs and didn't mess with them anymore. Then the officer said he was done for that time and took Melva back to her cell."

"Did Mrs. Bogardus say any more?" I asked.

"She may have but I … I had to leave. I, uh … felt a sneeze coming on."

"Uh-huh," I intoned. "And of course you couldn't just say excuse me and expect them to go on, could you?"

"Of course not. What kind of investigator does that?"

I chuckled at her indignant tone. "Okay. I need to finish my lunch. Can you transcribe all that for me and email it?"

"Yep. Will do, Emory. You have a great rest of your day, with taking Dr. Crawford home and all, and I'll try to see you tomorrow sometime."

"We'll do that. And Madison?"

"Yes?"

"Be careful with all of your … investigating."

"Yes'm." I could hear her smile. "I'll try."

Then we both disconnected.

CHAPTER 19

I WAS BUSSING MY TABLE WHEN MY PHONE RANG.

"Hi, AnnaMay." There are times it still seems strange to me to know who's called before they even say hello. But that's how my 'gift' works these days.

"Hi, Emory. How's everything going?"

"Good. Good stuff happening." I sat back down at my lunch table. "Jebbin comes home sometime late this afternoon. They said three, but I know not to trust that. Knowing hospitals, we won't actually be out the door until four or so. What's happening with you?"

My best friend laughed. "Good stuff happening, or good stuff found, to be more precise. It all *happened* in the mid 1800s. I've got all sorts of material for you to look through about early Twombly, the rich folks in town—other than the Twomblys themselves, that is—and the poor folk in town. I think there will be answers to a good many questions in all this stuff."

I couldn't help sighing. "It's all on paper, isn't it? And I'll have to come into the library to use it all, won't I?"

"Don't sound too glum, old chum. I've had my library minions run most of it through the big bed scanner, and I had them scan the more delicate items with the handheld scanner, so, mostly, it's all digitalized. Which, to be quite honest, we should have already done a long time ago. The whole collection should have been digitalized years ago. So that is a good thing happening. I've brought in some people from the Golden County Historical Society who know how to handle old documents, and we've begun the process of having everything preserved in digital format."

"Sounds wonderful, oh mighty Wizardess of the Library, but that doesn't totally answer my humble question, which I'll now rephrase. Are there still items I'll have to come to the library to look through?"

"Yes. There are a few items where I need to call in an expert before we scan them. Just to make sure they can take the handling. Even with the handheld units, you have to flatten the page fairly well to get a good, clear image, and that sort of thing can stress the bindings." AnnaMay laughed lightly. "Not too many things, though. Why? Is there a problem with coming in?"

"I don't think so." I sighed again. "I hadn't expected to feel this way, but I'm finding myself wanting to be at home more than I have been lately. So much of the summer I've been at the dig. Lately, I've been at the dig and the hospital. I was sort of looking forward to looking over the results of your concerted efforts while sitting comfortably in my jammies with a cup of tea and a snack nearby. I can't do that at the library."

We both laughed.

"No," the head librarian admitted. "Although we do have college students who come here in their jammies. And, before you say anything, yes, their jammies are not just casual clothes. I've asked them. But the food and drink, no. That has to stay at home." We laughed again, then she went on. "So, what do you want to do about seeing your treasures?"

I thought a few moments. "How's this? I would like to take a day off tomorrow. I mean a stay-at-home day. I'll come over to the library sometime on Monday to look at the stuff you're holding prisoner and pick up the digital stuff."

"That'll do just fine. I've got a really busy paperwork day today. Not a normal Saturday, so that will work best for me too."

"Thanks, Hon, for accommodating me and for doing all the research."

"Any time, m'dear. I hope getting Jebbin home goes smoothly and give my love to him and the Chatterjees."

"Will do."

I picked up my tray, took care of the things on it, and then headed up to Jebbin's room for the last time.

⌒

Jebbin was still asleep, all along the edge of his bed where they'd had him get out of it for his Walk About fitting. I took the other side and was soon asleep—or at least I assume I slept as I woke up to nurse Joan calling my name.

"Mrs. Crawford?"

"Hmm? Oh! Yes. Hi, Joan. Is it time to be getting ready?"

She smiled her chipper smile. "You bet it is. Word is that Tony will be up here in about half an hour and we're supposed to have Dr. Crawford's paperwork done and him all ready to head out the door when Tony gets here. One of the other nurses has started the paperwork part and I'm here to get you two up and going."

It was a rushed half hour, including the realization partway through that it wasn't going to be easy to get Jebbin into our VW Beetle. Thank goodness Tony had an SUV.

The drive home was short, but I almost pulled over and parked a few blocks short of the house. A wave of crawly tingles swarmed up my back and I had trouble paying attention to the road.

Sometimes the past won't stay in the past.

"Murder in the present comes before murder in the past," I said out loud, but the present and the past were getting tangled up, mingling together. Something Madison said. Something I'd read or heard somewhere else. In a flash of insight, I knew what I needed to do.

When I pulled up behind Tony's SUV in our driveway, I stuck my head out the window.

"Tony?" The big man was heading toward the porch to see if he could get someone to help us with Jebbin.

He turned to look at me. "Yeah?"

"I have to text a friend. She wanted to know when we got home. I'll only be a few seconds, and then I'll be ready to help."

"You got it, Mrs. Crawford."

I turned my attention to my phone.

AnnaMay, please send the digital stuff you have to me today. Can you email it?

Chatty, who had graciously left the lab for the occasion, came out of the house with Tony, and they carried my hubby up the porch steps, into our home, and deposited him in his recliner in our living room.

I was setting a glass of iced tea on Jebbin's chair-side table when AnnaMay's reply came through.

There's lots of stuff, all on a thumb drive. Will send a student-minion over with it after 6:00. You still coming in on Monday?

I tapped back: *Thanks for sending it over. Yes to Monday. See you then.*

I knew what I'd be doing later tonight.

We all ate in the living room off TV trays, so Jebbin wouldn't be by himself. We have one of those tables that extends over a bed, like they use in hospitals, and it worked beautifully for Jebbin in the recliner. He wouldn't have been able to have his leg up properly under the dining table. Deepti had a wonderful meal ready. Chicken Maakhani and Tandoori Shrimp, both served with Basmati rice, were our entrée choices accompanied by a salad of various fresh greens and chunks of mango tossed with a light fruity dressing, along with hot or iced chai to drink, made with Aine's wonderful blend. A scoop of pistachio ice cream that had been mixed with orange zest served in half a scooped-out orange was our refreshing dessert.

We had shared basic friendly talk as we enjoyed our meal, giving Tony a chance to get to know the Chatterjees. Deepti and Ragesh would be at our house much of the day while he was there. We were all well along in our conversation when Jebbin asked Tony a strange question.

"Tony, you're a physical therapist but you also do homecare. How are you with gross things getting discussed while you're eating?"

"Lord, Dr. Crawford." Tony laughed. "If I had problems with that I wouldn't weigh near as much as I do. You wouldn't believe what a lot of old folks talk about at meals."

We all laughed—and all of us but Tony knew what was coming.

"Alright. First, call me Jebbin."

"And me Emory," I cut in.

"Now, with you properly instructed and warned, Chatty and I are going to talk shop because I've been going nuts wondering what's been going on with the mummies and, now, with the party murder." Jebbin looked at Chatty. "Spill it, Chatterjee, or I'll have my personal aide here," he jabbed his thumb at Tony, "do some muscle manipulations that will get it out of you."

"I will be most cooperative, Jebbin." Chatty smiled his most charming smile. "Don't set your aide on me to do me harm. I will tell all I know most cheerfully."

Amid our laughter Deepti passed around the various serving dishes for second helpings and Chatty began spilling the beans.

"I was not expecting to have so much to do so soon. The mummies, while interesting, were not something that needed hurrying. But, with the sad shooting at the party last night, that has all changed, and I will be returning to the lab as soon as I finish both my recitation and my meal. My meal, which is most excellent and a shame to eat in such a hurry, my dearest wife."

Deepti smiled and bowed slightly to her husband. "My great pleasure, as always. Now please, what have you been up to at the lab?" Deepti was a fully licensed forensic lab tech and still worked at Chatty's lab whenever someone was on vacation or out sick, so all of the information would be of interest to her as well.

"Yeah, Dad. Have you seen the mummies? Are they cool lookin'?" Ragesh actually set his iPad aside to listen.

"Yes, I went to Antonia's lab at the hospital and looked at the mummies, and they look like mummies. If I am not mistaken, Emory has photos, yes?"

"Yes I do."

"There you are, Ragesh. Ask Aunt Emory later and you will see them for yourself. Then *you* can tell *me* if they are cool looking."

"Okay, Dad," said the lad. "Did you get to touch them or work on them?"

We all giggled a little at Ragesh's interrogation.

"May I tell my information about my day's work in my own way, son?" Chatty gently chided his boy.

"Yes, father," came the resigned reply. "But you take so long."

More laughter followed that.

"I will do my best to be quicker, not for your benefit, but because I have need to return to the lab, and I still need to finish my dinner." As he said this, Chatty added generous second helpings to his plate.

We waited, talking a bit more about the dig in general, until Chatty decided he'd eaten enough to take time out to talk.

"Well. As I have said, I went to the pathology lab at the hospital and met with Antonia. She had not done much more than look over the mummies because she had hurried back to Twombly when called about the shooting. That being the more important matter, she was dealing with that young man's bodily remains. She told me to help myself to the mummies and we would talk about Tom Knox's murder when she finished her examination."

Chatty finished his second entree and salad. Deepti got him one of the dessert cups, which he let sit to soften a little.

"The mummies are in excellent condition. It will be easy, I would say, to track the bullets' paths when all the calculations regarding the dehydration have been done. Both men had been shot in or very near to the heart. Since there is interest in which man might be the Melvin Sutton of the house's legend, Antonia said she will be searching for viable samples for DNA. I have heard," Chatty looked at me, "that the young lady who was arrested for the recent murder is a descendant of Melvin Sutton, so we have a known relation with whom to make a comparison. Antonia said that she requested samples from both the girl and her father, which were taken while he was present during the interviews at the police station."

The ice cream must have looked appropriately soft as Chatty paused to get a large spoonful. He savored it, as he does so often with the food he is served.

"This is most excellent, Deepti!"

She glowed at his praise. "Thank you, Nibodh."

He took a couple more spoonfuls before continuing.

"Where was I? Ah, yes. DNA. So, I have been running that today. It is a shame we don't know who the other man is ... once, that is, we have determined which of the mummies is Mr. Sutton. But, hopefully something will show up that can help with that as well. I have also asked Antonia to rehydrate the finger pads so we may get prints."

"Prints? Off surfaces that old?" I interrupted. "I mean, I know we can get the prints from the bodies, but compare them to what?"

Chatty smiled the smile of one in the know. "Ah, but we do have prints on some objects. Most important objects."

He paused. The infuriating man paused.

"Those being?" Jebbin raised an eyebrow at his colleague.

"The gun and the powder flask."

We all just stared.

"Powder flask?" Tony asked.

"For gun powder in old guns," Ragesh said.

Now we stared at Ragesh, who stared back at us like we were joking.

"You know. Old guns like muskets."

The light dawned on all us adults. I immediately thought of Madison. I am continually amazed at what comes out of the mouths of youngsters.

"Yeah." Ragesh looked at us all. "Yeah, you know. Well, they made pistols like that too. Pirate pistols and stuff were like that."

Chatty and Deepti were beaming with pride.

"Exactly, Ragesh!" Chatty praised his son. "All your interest in pirates has produced useful knowledge. If you like, I will take you to see the small pistol and its flask and ramrod. But it will need to wait until I am not so busy. Please, do not let me forget to show them to you." He turned his attention back to the rest of us. "The flask in particular has a few excellent looking prints. It is made of brass that is not highly polished or lacquered and has therefore oxidized the prints. From that, we should be able to determine which man did the shooting ... or, if both used the gun."

I thought, not for the first time since I fell into the amateur sleuthing, that maybe I shouldn't be holding things back. Like, say for instance, the pocketwatch. As things seemed to be getting easier and easier, I dismissed my concern.

Chatty had moved on to the shooting at the party.

"Antonia analyzed the boy's stomach contents, and of course, I've been running tests as well. What she found, and I confirmed just before I quit to welcome my good friend home and to enjoy a most wonderful dinner, is that the mystery drink is distilled liquor made from corn. Moonshine."

I hoped no one heard my gulp.

"Antonia told me anyone with some knowledge, equipment, and the use of the internet can make it, but that she knew the police were going to be looking at Larry Suter. Apparently he does have a permit to make it and to sell it at his restaurant. He is also the father of the young lady whom they suspect of the murder," Chatty said looking at Jebbin and me. "Isn't he?"

Chapter 20

CHATTY CHATTED ON ABOUT THE BALLISTICS FROM THE PARTY MURDER, but I was only half listening. He said he'd have his final conclusions first thing tomorrow morning, so my head knew it wasn't missing any important information right now.

My head held onto the word MOONSHINE.

Moonshine and Larry Suter.

Moonshine and Melva.

Moonshine and how very drunk young people were getting at the secret parties out in the boonies of Golden County.

Madison had said that Mrs. Bogardus had told Jairus that the Suters had both paled when the officer doing their interview had mentioned the "high octane booze". I shook my head to clear up that last thought. It reminded me of junior high school with all of its 'so-and-so said so-and-so said' stuff.

Chatty's mention of moonshine had done it. His mention of that unique something that set The Coal Bin apart from other bar-restaurant combinations in the area.

Larry Suter sells moonshine in his establishment.

Mind, as Chatty said, Larry does have the permit the state requires for him to make and sell his family's treasured recipe. But moonshine *is* available at The Coal Bin. It's featured on the menu and on a sign above the bar, '*Moonshine made from our 200-year-old family recipe!*' But it isn't mentioned in his newspaper, TV, or radio advertising, so most people, except Coal Bin regulars, forget about it—like I had. It's expensive as well, with a two shots per customer limit. Permit holders are only allowed to make a certain amount each year, so I guess the two shot limit helps each night's allotment last.

I also reckoned that the Sheriff's Department had considered a possible connection between very strong liquor at secret parties and the moonshine-making owner of The Coal Bin before the shooting happened. But they had let Larry walk out after the interview, so they must not have any solid proof that it was his moonshine being served at the parties. At least, no proof yet. Who knew what the lab's analysis would be able to show.

And where did Melva fit in with all of this?

Madison had intended to get a sample of the stuff while she was at the party. Had she managed it?

The doorbell rang.

"I'll get it," I said as I got up off the end of my chaise where I'd been sitting to better use a TV tray for dinner. It was, as I hoped it might be, AnnaMay's student worker with the thumb drive. I thanked her and stuffed it into my jeans pocket. There would be time to look at it later after the Chatterjees left and Tony and I got Jebbin tucked into bed.

It was a little after nine o'clock when I sat my rear in my usual chair at my kitchen table with a cup of Aine's Discernment tea steaming in my *Fiddles are happy violins!* mug.

The Chatterjees had left around eight and then Jebbin declared he was tired. It took nearly an hour to get him into bed. Tony said it would get shorter as Jebbin improved and could use his Walk About more often, and it would be even better when his wrist was healed enough to lose the cast. Tony had bid me good night and headed to the guest room as I headed to the kitchen.

My laptop was booted up and I plugged the thumb drive from AnnaMay into a USB port. I took a couple of sips of my tea as the drive connected and I clicked on the icon to open it. If I'd been hoping to also find intriguing tidbits about either AnnaMay Langstock or the Twombly College and City Library on that drive, I would have been disappointed. Nothing was on it but one folder titled: *1844 Golden Co - Twombly and Sutton House.*

A flash of an image, the watch I found under the desk in Melvin and Polly's bedroom, came and went. Not a vision or anything that dramatic, just a normal mental image.

I double clicked the folder's icon. There were four folders inside it:
Maps and Plats
Important Families
1844 Headlines From Golden Co Gazette
As well as articles directly relating to Sutton House Flood.

One of the maps I'd looked at before, the one with *Sutton farms here* written on it, floated before my mind's eye. Strange. I often get mental pictures, I think most of us do, but these felt different. Maybe this was how Discernment tea worked?

I opened the *Maps and Plats* folder.

There were several .jpg images and one Word document labeled, *Look here first.*

So I looked there first.

Hi Emory,

I've the feeling these aren't going to give you what you're wanting. I know they didn't give me what I wanted. There is nothing on any map, and more suspiciously, nothing on any of the plats, that indicates who owned the land the Suttons sharecropped. MOST UNUSUAL! Even back in that day, even out here on the prairies, land ownership was well documented. It is very strange that a tract of land with farm buildings and a residence on it has no indication of ownership. As you'll see from the plats in particular, and even on some of the maps, the owner's name is frequently printed within the boundaries of the land they own.

Neither I nor any of the students I had helping with this task found anything that showed who the owner of that quarter section was.

I don't have access to the city or county records, though, and it could be—should be—in those records. The sale had to have been registered with Golden County, and all those papers are kept at the county courthouse in Twombly—which is where the records should still be rather than in our collection at the library.

Unless ... I just thought of something.

This could have all been done under-the-table. The land could have been used to pay a bribe, pay off a debt, or even (rather common back in the day) used as a bid and lost in a card game. In any of these cases, there wouldn't be a record.

My servants (student workers) and I will keep dredging here. I suggest you try the courthouse.

I ran out of time to do more than cursory examinations of the materials in the other files. Mostly just looked at enough to determine if they'd have anything of use in the articles and such.

Shall we get together on Monday?

Good luck!

AnnaMay

I finished the letter with my mind full of swirling images. The gold watch we'd found with the initials *R.L.W.* surfaced again. The page in Polly's diary with the initial *R.* in a passage where she was referring to Melvin and the boys perhaps not doing all the work they should have been doing on the farm they sharecropped.

I saw rain and high water blocking dirt roads, washing them away. Black water. Swirling water. Washing away crops, and barns, and grain bins.

And sinking a house.

CHAPTER 21

THE CLOCK BY MY BEDSIDE READ 8:12 IN GLOWING RED DIGITS, AND I heard someone moving around in the kitchen. I listened. I heard music and talking as well. Popular music of India and speaking in ... well, the Indian language the Chatterjees speak, which I think is Hindi but might be one of the other languages of that ancient land.

I smiled and relaxed. Deepti and Ragesh had arrived and all was well with my world. I assumed that Chatty was already at the lab.

Jebbin had needed a bathroom visit during the night, which, of course, woke me up as well, but that was okay. It was going to be part of the pattern of our lives for a few months at least. He had called Tony in, they had taken care of everything, and I was able to get back to sleep shortly after Jebbin was tucked back in.

"You awake?" my dear man mumbled.

I rolled over and snuggled up to his left side. "Yep."

"I'd put my arm around you but I'm afraid I'd knock you in the head with my cast. Lightweight and removable it may be, but it's still clumsy."

"That's okay, Hon. It's not forever and if it was, I'd learn to deal with it."

We snuggled and talked for a while until both of us needed to respond to our bladders. While Jebbin called for Tony, I got up, wiggled into my bathrobe, and grabbed some clothes for the day before heading for the all-purpose bathroom that was off the hallway that led from the kitchen to the hallway where all the bedrooms are.

I had fallen asleep at the kitchen table last night, head resting on my laptop's keyboard. At 11:30 I woke enough to toddle off to our room, take off my shoes, socks, and jeans, and fall into bed. If I ever use Discernment tea again, I won't let it steep as long. I'm certain all that mental imagery was what had knocked me out, so to speak. All that aside, I was wide awake now and wondering what the day was going to bring.

"Ah! You are awake at last," Deepti said with a smile as I walked into the kitchen. "I have prepared a breakfast casserole. Such wonderful things they are. I made it yesterday afternoon and it has been in the refrigerator. I will preheat the oven and we will be ready to eat shortly."

She turned toward the stove with a swirl of her dupatta, set the oven going, then turned back to me. "Would you like coffee? Perhaps tea or chai? And there are sweet rolls and doughnuts available."

I smiled and laughed. "You're going to make me get pudgier, Deepti. Tempting me with all those goodies. I'll have some of the chai, please."

"It is for Sunday morning only. I have learned from friends who are Christians that it is often the case that Sunday meals have more food available than weekday meals. That it is part of it being a day of rest and celebration of your faith. Tomorrow, there won't be as much food." Her eyes sparkled with mischief. "So, if you begin to gain weight while I am here cooking, it will not be entirely my fault."

"Yes, you're right, Deepti, it is our holy day and a day of rest and celebration. Thank you for thinking of it. But I still might blame you for my waistline getting bigger." I gave her a wink, which set her laughing again.

I didn't have the heart to tell her we usually did a larger meal only at mid-day. And who was I to turn down a nice, full breakfast?

I was sitting at the dining table … Deepti had thought the bigger table might be best with Jebbin's leg to be considered so she'd set that table for breakfast … halfway through a scrumptious cinnamon roll and my first mug of Chai, when the text alert sounded from my phone. I hopped up to get my phone from the small counter in the kitchen next to the doors out to the screened in porch. It was from AnnaMay.

I mentioned a Mon. get together in letter on drive. Your nosiness is rubbing off on me. Can you make it over to my kingdom today?

I replied: *You were already nosey.* ☺ *1:00 or 2:00?*

1:30 ;-) I'll be down in the Archives Room. Just knock & I'll let you in.

Deepti was putting the casserole in the oven and Jebbin and Tony had just come into the kitchen when I looked up.

"Jebbin!"

He was walking with his Walk About.

"Ta Da! How about this, huh? When's our next jam session? I'm ready for some cloggin'."

"Yeah, right." I smirked. "You'll be doing good to stand up and hold that heavy banjo of yours. But, it sure is good to see you without a wheelchair, Hon."

His beautiful Kat Eyz copper-plated banjo weighs twenty pounds. I figured that for now, seeing as he still has strains and sprains to recover from, holding his own weight up was more than enough to ask. Tony helped Jebbin sit at the head of the table.

"Head of the table for the head of the house," he said with a wink. "That and no one's sitting across from him to get poked in their knees by the leg part of the unit."

Jebbin's foot, in its walking cast, rested comfortably on the floor.

Tony addressed his charge with authority. "Now, Jebbin. You pay attention to how your foot feels right now. It's happy right now so how you sense it feeling is your foot doing good. You start to feel any prickles, tingles, mad crazy itches, or cramps, and we take the unit off and prop your lower leg upright then. Is that clear?"

"Yes, sir." Jebbin replied with a salute.

"You got it." He smacked Jebbin companionably on the shoulder and sat down in the chair to his left.

"Breakfast is nearly ready!" Deepti called from the kitchen and I went to help bring things to the table.

The casserole had ham, onions, and cheeses along with the bread base. There was a bowl of cubed mixed fruits with blackberries and raspberries mixed in. We brought the box of sweet rolls and doughnuts in as well. Jebbin said grace, giving thanks not only for the wonderful meal but also for his being hurt as slightly as he had been and for all the friends and medical folks who were doing so much to help us both.

We had started to pass our plates to Deepti when Chatty burst in the front door.

"Ah! My timing is impeccable, as always. I am starving." He sat in the only empty chair at the table, grabbed and took a bite out of a Danish, chewing it as he dished mixed fruit onto his plate.

Then he stopped, the spoon of fruit halfway from the bowl to his plate. He looked over at Jebbin who was giving him a reproving look.

"Ahem. Dr. Chatterjee?" intoned Professor Crawford.

Chatty blushed as much as his complexion allowed while hastily swallowing the bite of Danish. "Yes?"

"Weren't we called on the carpet about digging into a meal in a thoughtless rush on another occasion when you were here helping at the lab?"

Both men looked at me.

I nodded with royal grace. "You were indeed. You owe your good wife better manners, Dr. Chatterjee."

Deepti was chuckling behind her hand as Nibodh slowly added the spoonful of fruit to his plate before setting the plate down and turning to her.

"My most humble apologies, my dear. You have made a glorious breakfast, and I shall be my usual appreciative self and savor it. May I pass my plate for some ... whatever that is that you are serving to everyone?"

"Breakfast casserole," she explained, "and yes, you may."

"I am greatly sorry for my hurrying." Chatty looked around at the rest of us. "Especially to you, Ragesh. That was not a good example to set for you."

"It's okay, Dad." The boy grinned. "Nice to know you're not perfect." We all laughed, then Ragesh continued, "But I bet you have some big news, or you wouldn't be so wound up. You do, don't you?"

"I do indeed. I have checked and double checked my results of the ballistics."

"And?" Jebbin leaned forward as he asked.

Chatty milked his moment for all it was worth, but finally answered.

"The bullet from the gun Melva Suter was holding when she was taken in does not match the bullet that killed Tom Knox. She did not shoot the young man. I sent word of this to the Sheriff's Department last night at 10:30, as soon as I was certain of my findings. It is my hope they let Miss Suter go home late last night, but they should most definitely do so this morning as there is now no reason for them to hold her."

A wave of relief swept over me.

"Then who did shoot him?" Ragesh asked.

"That," his father answered, "is the next problem. I know the gun young Melva had in her hand is a Smith & Wesson .38, since we have the gun itself. The gun Tom Knox had was the same make and caliber. It is a rather common gun. The bullet that killed the young man is a 9mm that could have come from a couple of different guns made by different manufacturers. I have sent all the photos and the details of that bullet to a friend who is more expert with guns and ammunition than I. Hopefully we will hear from him by Tuesday or Wednesday."

"Let's finish our breakfast, Chatty," Jebbin said. "Then we can head over to the lab. We can't do much more with the ballistics results, but there are further tests we can do on the moonshine, and then we can get some work done on the two mummies from the house."

"You are able to work, my friend?"

Jebbin held up his right hand and wiggled his fingers. "One handed, but I should be able to do some of the tests." He nodded at Tony. "I'll bring my helper with me, so we won't need to interrupt your work."

"I won't be here either," I said. "Well, not this afternoon at least."

Everyone looked at me.

"I got a text from AnnaMay before breakfast, and we're meeting at the library at one-thirty to look over material that can't leave the Archives Room. These are things we're hoping might shed some light on the mystery at the house. You know, who the other mummy is, since it's fairly likely that at least one of them is Melvin Sutton."

Deepti spoke up. "That will work very well as Ragesh was wishing to go swimming at the Twombly pool this afternoon."

"You sure are a busy bunch." Tony shook his head.

We finished our wonderful meal. The men all left for the lab with Tony pushing Jebbin in the wheelchair across campus, while I helped Deepti clean up. Then, since it was only around 10:30, Ragesh and I pulled out our fiddles, and I started teaching him to play by ear—a vital part of bluegrass and folk music.

CHAPTER 22

ANNAMAY AND I STOOD SIDE BY SIDE AT A TABLE IN THE SOFTLY LIT ARCHIVES Room of the Twombly College and City Library. The library was open but not overly busy, as is typical for Sunday afternoons. The morning had been foggy and clammy, but by the time I headed over to AnnaMay's kingdom, the sun was shining brightly even though the breeze still chilled my bones despite my jeans, flannel shirt, and jacket. At least we were having another break from the rain.

"This is what I'm dying to dig into." AnnaMay swept her arm to indicate the three wooden crates that sat on the table. They were all about two feet long, a foot and a half wide, and a foot deep. "As far as I know," she continued, "these haven't been opened since they arrived at the library in the 1950s sometime. They are from the old Westford mansion."

"Hmm. A 'W' name."

"Does that mean something to you, Emory?"

I grinned. "Possibly. Let me avoid saying too much until I know a little more. Like, who are the Westfords? When our family first moved here, I had a lot of fun learning the history of Twombly and Golden County, remember? That's how we got to be friends. I was hanging out at the library a lot and asking so many questions. But I don't remember that name. You said 'mansion' so I'm assuming they were wealthy."

"Yes, they were. Here." AnnaMay handed me one of two pry bars that were sitting on the table. "Have at it." She continued talking as we worked the tops off the crates. "At one time I think Phineas Reginald Westford was giving Jairus Aiden Merriweather Twombly the First some real competition for the claim of wealthiest man in Golden County. Quite a feat, seeing as Jairus I was the first to buy land in the area, started the town, and was able to have the county named with his wife's middle name."

We both worked on the last crate, and finally all three sat open.

Whatever was in them had been well packed in excelsior—thin spaghetti-like wood shavings used to cushion fragile items.

We dug in.

"My version of an archeological dig," AnnaMay proclaimed. "No weather to contend with. No dirt or mud. No insects buzzing around. Just a clean, climate-controlled room and cotton gloves."

She handed a pair of gloves to me.

"You're missing all the fun," I chided her.

We started gently unpacking old books and bundles wrapped in butcher's paper and tied with twine.

"I'm thinking these were either packed up in the mid 1800s, when the family suddenly went into a decline, or perhaps after the Civil War when they sold the house and moved to Quincy, Illinois."

"Quincy?" I asked. "Why Quincy?"

"They already had holdings and a Mississippi River shipping business there that, unlike their various endeavors here in Golden County, were doing quite well. Well, what do we have?" AnnaMay and I looked at the items from the crates.

Without even saying anything, we had sorted the items in the same manner. I had a pile of books and a pile of wrapped packets, and so did AnnaMay.

I counted in my head. "I have seven books and five variously shaped parcels."

"I've got six books and nine parcels. Since this is my realm, as Queen of the Library, I say we start with the books, then the parcels that could be packets of papers—judging by their shape—and then the parcels that could be anything because their shapes are all different."

"And I agree."

AnnaMay spoke as we each reached for a book. "We do have a Westford section in the reference library and a small section for them here in the archives. Mostly, they are the sort of thing well-to-do folks often leave for posterity. Phineas wrote a good many of those. They're diaries that are full of the good and important things he and his family had done for the area, but alas, they include none of the problems and day-to-day things that most historians actually find more valuable. These, however, look more personal. I have a handwritten cookbook here." She waved a faded and slightly water-stained booklet at me.

"And I have a *Child's Garden of Verses*. Fairy tales, poems, and such."

We each kept opening and skimming through books.

"BINGO!"

I jumped at my friend's sudden exclamation in the quiet room.

"Lucky," I said. "I hardly have any of my squares marked."

"Very funny. I've found a small diary and I think it might have been Phineas's."

"Really?"

AnnaMay moved the small book over so we both could see it.

"Notice how clear his handwriting is?" She ran a gloved index finger under a line of straight, even, beautifully written words.

"Yes, a wonderful example of Copperplate script, otherwise known as English Roundhand. He must have been raised in a wealthy family and been well schooled."

AnnaMay seemed surprised at my response.

"What? I used to do calligraphy, remember?"

"I did remember, but all I remember you using was italic, Celtic, and various Gothics."

I chuckled. "Well done! You remembered all that. I never did try Copperplate or Spencerian, which came after it here in the U.S. And, what you mean by Celtic is actually called Uncial."

"Yes, yes," she hurried on. "Lovely handwriting. Phineas was from a well-to-do family in Philadelphia. I pointed it out more because it makes it so much easier to read."

"So read some of it."

AnnaMay cleared her throat and began reading an entry.

September 5, 1835

Once again I am having to appease the wrath of a neighbor in order to keep Reginald out of trouble. He tempted Mr. Sampson's eight year old lad to gamble at cards with him, quickly winning the young lad's favorite toy. Then, he apparently intimidated the boy in order to keep knowledge of the affair from Mr. Sampson.

I do not know what shall become of my boy. The usual punishments of a paddling, being sent to his room without a meal, being made to remain in the house instead of being with other children, and the like have not cured him of his wildness and disregard for rules. His disobedience was bad enough when he was younger, but now that he is 13 years of age, it is all the more disturbing to me.

At least, thus far, there appears to be little of meanness in his actions, only the, by him called, "fun" of his "games." He cannot resist a risk or a challenge. Nor can he resist pulling others into things with him.

I waited until AnnaMay was finished.

"Reginald. His son's initials would have been R.W. then," I softly said.

"Yes. They would be." She gave me a long look. "Out with it, Crawford. You have one of your looks on your face."

"First, can we look at a later entry? One when Reginald would be older?"

She gently opened the pages at the end of the book, and then worked back until she reached one with writing.

May 12, 1844

"Well," she said looking up at me. "Can't do much better than the same year as the flood, can we?"

"I guess not. Read on."

> *Once more I have grave concerns about Reginald.*
> *It has come to my attention that he might be involved in some shady dealings with the man who farms the land by where the creeks converge, one Melvin Sutton, who is Reginald's elder by, I would estimate, close to ten years.*

I reached into the long-strapped, crocheted hobo bag I'd brought with me. I'd stuffed wallet, camera, binoculars, and a few other items into it. One item, which was wrapped in a washcloth inside a Tupperware container, I pulled out of the bag. "Have a look at this."

My friend popped open the seal, then carefully removed and unwrapped the R.L.W. pocketwatch.

"Okay. Where did you get this?" As soon as she asked she put her hand up to stop my answer. "Nope. No need to speak. You brought it out of the Sutton House."

I wasn't about to look contrite. "Yes. I did. Well, Madison

Twombly and Melva Suter and I brought it and a few other things out, yes. I know Dr. Koerner well. He's more interested in the house itself than the men inside it. After all, they didn't make it sink. He's quite content to let people like Jebbin and Chatty bother with them. Melva is a Sutton descendant and she wanted to bring the things we found up so that they wouldn't just get shoved away in …" I gestured at the things on the table, "crates and boxes somewhere. Pry the cover open." I added.

She did.

She gasped. For the first time since I've known her, AnnaMay Langstock looked shaken.

"It's his!"

"Could've been some other guy with R.W. for first and last initials." I was casual with the reply, but the shocked look that stayed on her face made me wish I hadn't been so flippant.

"No. No, Emory, it's his. I happen to know that his middle name was Leander." She looked up from the watch, held it toward me, and whispered, "R.L.W."

CHAPTER 23

WE STARED AT EACH OTHER FOR SEVERAL MOMENTS.

Wide eyed, AnnaMay spoke first. "Reginald Leander Westford! The wastrel son of Jairus the First's main competitor?" The next moment, the shock in her eyes was replaced with urgency. "Yes. Yes. Yes."

She reached for a laptop computer that I hadn't noticed on the table. "Oh, yes, yes. The *Gazette* articles we scanned. The ones I sent you copies of. Did you read any of them?"

"No. I didn't get past the *Maps* folder, since you did say read that one first. I ... ah, kinda had ... well, let's just say I was really tired and fell asleep on my laptop keyboard after reading your note."

AnnaMay gave me one of her staff sergeant looks. "Messing about with Aine's teas again?" She waved off any attempt at an answer and turned back to the laptop. "Never mind. All's well. I just remember noticing ... Here."

She turned the machine so we could both see the screen.

"A *Golden County Gazette* article dated July ninth, 1844—three days after the flood and two days after it was discovered the house was missing."

More To July 6ᵗʰ Flood Than Just A Missing House

There are more mysteries in Golden County in the wake of the horrific flood that caused widespread destruction throughout the low lands along the Okaw and Rock Creeks.

Along with the expected remains of buildings, waterlogged and ruined personal possessions, and dead animals, the lengthy trail of debris along the creeks has included as many as three swollen and battered corpses, none of which have yet been identified. It is, perhaps, too early for word of missing persons to have gotten to our offices in Twombly, or to the sheriff's office, but until such desperate pleas to find missing loved ones become known, there is little chance of discovering who the poor lost souls are.

If you are reading this copy of the Golden Co. Gazette, *whether you live within Golden County, or up stream from our borders, please endeavor to report any information you may have concerning missing loved ones of your own or any such inquiries you have been made aware of by friends or neighbors.*

"O ... kay." I drew out the word. "And why is this important? We know where our two men were."

"Yes. But, what is very important here is that the Westfords are V.I.P.s, yet no report had come in about Reginald being missing."

I closed my eyes and sighed. "Well duh, Emory." I opened my eyes to look at my friend. "Yes. I should have caught that myself. Was their mansion close enough to Twombly that news could have made it in? Was it near the creeks, and if so, which side was it on?"

"It *is* on the town side of the creeks, just like the Twombly mansion," AnnaMay explained. "As things go in rural areas, they were neighbors. The Westfords lived a mile and a half south-south-west of the Twomblys."

"So you'd think they would have been in a panic and sent inquiries to town at least by the evening of the seventh or morning of the eighth."

"I agree, but then, I had noticed this article …" She flipped and flicked through items on the screen. "This one here, dated July thirteenth."

Fate of Son of Local Cattle Magnate is Known

Word has come from Mr. Phineas Reginald Westford regarding his youngest son, Mr. Reginald Leander Westford.

Rumors were abroad that the young man, twenty-two years of age, had been swept away and lost to his loved ones in the devastating flood of six nights ago, leaving behind his young wife and, as yet, unborn child.

A letter to the editor of this fine newspaper from Mr. P. Westford confirms that Mr. Reginald and his wife, the former Miss Ester Donnelly of Quincy, had been sent (with a manservant and ladies' maid) to oversee the family shipping business, Westford & Sons Shipping, located along the Mississippi River near the town of Quincy, Illinois, with word arriving this very morning via a courier that the couple had indeed arrived at the home of Mrs. Westford's parents, where they were expected to live until obtaining a home of their own.

However, we are deeply saddened to report that further news concerning the young Mr. & Mrs. Westford is not good. Young Mr. Reginald had become ill on the journey and died the day after their arrival at the Donnelly home.

Mrs. Westford has taken to her bed and is expected to remain in Quincy, at the very least, until her child is born.

Mr. Reginald Leander Westford will be buried in the Donnelly family cemetery.

Condolences and messages of sympathy may be sent to Messrs.

Tomlinson & Williams, the Westford family solicitors, and will be forwarded to Mr. & Mrs. Westford.

I stared at the writing on the screen.

"They lied."

"Yes." AnnaMay's tone harmonized with my own. "They lied."

AnnaMay printed off the articles for me.

"I had wondered about all this after I read it." She shook her head as the printer whirred. "I had wondered why more wasn't written about Reginald's death. That article is the only mention of it. Funerals were a big deal in that day, yet there are no reports about a grand funeral with all the upper crust of Quincy in attendance. From what I know from reading Phineas's official diaries, he wouldn't normally have passed up an opportunity like this to get his family's name in the papers, or the weeks of emotional outpouring either. But these two short bits are all there is."

"You're right, of course. But now we know. He had no idea where his son was, other than his concerns that he was up to something with Melvin." I didn't mention Melvin's secret diary I'd found in his desk in the house and shared with Melva and Madison—the one that spoke of digging and needing lumber for bracing.

AnnaMay tucked the printouts into a stiff mailing envelope and handed them to me. I stuck them in my hobo bag along with the Tupperware container with Reginald's watch in it.

"That last entry in the little diary makes it sound like Phineas thought Melvin was leading Reginald astray." She picked up the small book, caressing its cover with a book lover's gentle fingers. "But I think he knew better. Or he might have thought that they were in on something equally." She looked me in the eye. "Do you think they would have been in on something together as equals?"

I shook my head. "No. I have the feeling Reginald might have owned the land Melvin sharecropped, and there's no way someone like Reginald would have ever felt a sharecropper was his equal. Not even in something underhanded."

"I think you're right on that." With a little sigh, she set Phineas's sad diary about his wayward boy back on the table. "Are you done for today?"

"Yeah. I have my camera and binoculars in my bag. I think I'll go out to Sutton's Lake and see if the birds are as cold as I'll be."

We hugged goodbye, and then she walked me to the door to the Archives Room.

"Be careful, Emory."

"I always try to be."

When I got to the door into the main library I glanced back.

AnnaMay was still watching me from the Archive Room's partially open door.

CHAPTER 24

TIMES LIKE THIS, I DOUBTED MY SANITY.

It wasn't freezing at the lake; it was in the mid sixties, but because of the prairie wind it was a bit nippy to be out watching birds. Not that I hadn't been out there in the dead of winter with temperatures below freezing—I had—but I had been dressed for it.

Then again, perhaps part of my chill today was my mood.

After a small bit of walking up and down the east-west road out of Twombly I got back in my car and looked out over the blue, sparkling lake with the oddly wide shoreline.

I was parked on a short pull-off that had been created with a layer of gravel to accommodate one of the two cars belonging to dig team members. First come, first served. The rest of us parked along the edge of the road wherever the shoulder was wide enough between the asphalt and the drainage ditches. Strangely, the pull-off was nearly in line with the house. The pavilion over the hole in its roof was slightly off to my left. I smiled at the thought of how many times we had parked there wondering where the house might be buried, and we had practically been staring right at it.

Next to me in the pull-off was a county sheriff's cruiser. The road was no longer being blocked, too many people used it to get in to work in Twombly, but the site was still being guarded.

After about ten more minutes, I backed out and turned the nose of the Beetle to the west. Left at the crossroad and down another road was a small pond across from Rock Lake that had also been created by gravel quarrying. The birds liked it there, too.

An older model, dingy SUV was pulled into what was left of an access road from when the quarry was active. As I drew near, the passenger window went down and Madison Twombly waved enthusiastically for me to pull in. I lowered my window as I did so.

"Way cool that you showed up, Emory!" Madison smiled happily. "They let Melva out around six this morning and she texted me around eleven to see if I'd want to come out here with her. We were just thinking of calling you. Did you have a feeling to come here?"

Well, now that she mentioned it …

"Yes. I guess I did. I knew late this morning that I wanted to come out here when I was done meeting with AnnaMay Langstock, so I packed my bird watching stuff."

"Again, cool!" She laughed. "Come on over. We have snacks and sorta hot coffee."

I shut off the Bug, grabbed my hobo bag, and got into the backseat of their vehicle.

"I'm so glad to see you're out, Melva." I reached over and gave her shoulder a squeeze. "Dr. Chatterjee, the forensic scientist who helps Jebbin when he needs help, told us at breakfast this morning that he told the sheriffs last night that the gun you had wasn't the one used to shoot Tom."

"Yeah." Her smile was weak, but it was a smile. "I wish I'd never … well, wishing doesn't change a damn … I mean darn … thing.

Tom is gone. I'm just so glad I didn't actually do it. Ya know? Dad took me over to The Coal Bin and made breakfast for us both. He was so glad to have me home. We don't open till twelve-thirty on Sundays so it was just us and the kitchen prep staff."

"Where'd you get the wheels, Melva?" Madison wasn't old enough to drive and Melva was in the driver's seat, so it wasn't hard to figure out who had driven them here. But Melva had always been dropped off at the dig, and needed rides home.

My question made the girl uncomfortable. "Dad didn't know if I'd be out today or not." She looked out at the pond, not at me. "So he scheduled someone else for my usual shift this afternoon. I asked him if I could get together with Madison and he said yeah, as long as he knew where we'd be. So I told him, and that's where we are."

There was a great deal of the old, uptight, full-of-attitude Melva back in her voice and body language.

"Makes sense," I said, trying to maintain a neutral tone. "Why here though? There's no dig going on today."

"Yeah. I know that. Duh." Melva sneered. "Little Miss Madison texted and said we should come out here, so, yeah. We're here."

Madison jumped in. "I had a ... feeling of my own that ..."

Melva cut her off. But her voice was quiet. The hard edge was gone.

"I've heard about the Twomblys." She looked over at Madison. "They say you guys know things before they happen sometimes, and that you have ways to get people to do what you want them to. Is it true?"

"Yes."

There was silence, and I sat amazed at Madison's answer. These things weren't usually up for discussion by the Twomblys.

"Not, I'm sure, quite the way you've heard," Madison continued. "We aren't witches or wizards or anything like that. Just something that runs in our family like hair color or skin tone or being able to sing well. And we sure can't make people do things they don't want to do. It's just that we can be good at persuading people. In nice ways, that is."

Melva nodded, but said nothing. She said nothing for a full minute.

I watched the clock on the dash.

"I guess it is real then," she finally said. "I've been wanting to talk to you guys ever since I sobered up after ... Well, yeah, you know. They let me out really early this morning. Some guy with Schneider on his badge got really snotty with me, tellin' me I was damn lucky the bullet didn't match but they all knew I was into this party and gambling stuff somehow, and they'd be keeping a really close eye on me."

"I know that officer," Madison growled. "He's meaner than ..."

"He's right."

Madison and I stared at Melva.

"He's right, and they're gonna find out, and I'm gonna be in for it bad."

She turned in her seat, resting her back against the driver's side door, so she could see us easier.

"I started gambling on the machines at The Coal Bin. I'd sneak over at night and play 'em. I've had a key since I was twelve." She stared at her hands—her right index finger nail pick, pick, picking at her left thumbnail. "That got to be ... not enough, ya know? I was already running with the rough kids at school, and I'd heard talk of real gambling in town. So I made friendly with the ones doing the talking, and soon I was there as often as I could get away from the stupid Coal Bin. Dad was always too busy and ..."

She sniffed and a tear crept down her face.

"Trusting. He trusted me 'cause I'd been such a good kid when Mom was around. But everything had changed. I wasn't Mom's girl anymore. I felt ... felt like I wasn't anybody's anything ... 'cept when

I was at the games. Then … then I was this adult-like person who was making her own decisions and making money and …"

She looked out the windshield at the small lake. A duck took off from the water and she followed its flight until it was out of sight.

"And I was being an ass." She looked up, an embarrassed blush on her cheeks. "A fool. A jerk." She looked back down at her hands. "I need to clean up my language, I think. Anyway, I wasn't being anything like I thought I was, and when I started losing more than winning, it all fell apart. That bas … creep, Pete. He runs the games and he runs the parties. He runs a lot of what's bad around Golden County and some of the other counties around here, too. I was into him so deep I'd never be able to pay it back. But he came up with another idea instead of money."

The spiders ran up my back. I shivered. A knowing.

"Moonshine," Madison and I said in stereo.

Melva stared, open-mouthed.

Madison patted Melva's arm, care for her friend shining in her eyes. "There ya go. Intuition in action."

"It makes sense," I gently added, feeling a bit Holmesian, like Aine. "Your dad has a permit and sells it at The Coal Bin. It's quite a novelty and has a bad, rowdy reputation. Things that would appeal to thrill-seeking young people."

"Yeah. That's kinda what Pete said to me. He said he knew it would be a big draw. Then he said it was only till I paid back what I owed him, but I think that was just a line. He kept me gambling and I kept on losing too often, so I had to keep on making the 'shine for him."

There was another long pause.

"That was why I … um. I didn't want to go find that place described in Grandpa Melvin's secret book. You guys remember? The one in the stand of trees?"

Madison and I both nodded.

"I already knew where it was and what he was doing, not the *why* he was doing it, but the *what*. It's a tunnel and it's where I set up my still."

"You set up a still in a tunnel? That's dangerous!" I was instantly sorry I raised my voice.

"I'm not stupid!" Melva yelled back at me, way too loudly for the confines of the SUV. "I put in a vent system, which was a lotta hard work. And I use propane instead of wood. I know how to solder copper tubing and how to look for leaks. It's perfectly safe."

I held up my hands in surrender. "Okay. Okay. I'm sorry. I didn't mean that you're stupid. It's just that I'm married to a chemist, and I know stuff like that is dangerous in enclosed spaces." I took a deep breath and let it out. "I was just concerned about you, that's all, Hon."

Melva took a breath of her own and nodded. "Yeah. Okay. Sorry. Anyway." She took another breath. "I want to show you guys, but it has to be at night and even then it could be tricky with the dig site being watched. And there's something more."

She took a few seconds to look each of us in the eye. She must have been comfortable with what she saw there because she went on.

"I have proof that Pete is the one who made me make the stuff and I hid it down there. I got video with audio on a memory card and prints too of him picking up full jugs and loading them into his truck. He always tells me how good the 'product' is, how much had come off what I owed him, and that I'd better keep it coming if I knew what was good for me and my dad. So it's plenty clear I wasn't just selling him the stuff on my own for my own profit. I hid a remote control camera where it would get the whole pickup.

"It's all in an old metal tackle box near where the still is. I want to get it and take it to the cops, turn myself in, and tell them everything I know about Pete. I don't want the cops coming for me, maybe arresting me, while I'm working at The Coal Bin or at the dig. Haulin' me off in front of everyone. I want to do it myself the way

I want to do it." She looked out the windshield again. "Not some way that will just embarrass my dad even worse than I already have."

Madison broke the thoughtful silence. "Can you do the driving, Emory? So Melva doesn't have to … um, borrow her dad's SUV?"

I grinned. "You mean so she doesn't have to add borrowing the vehicle to sneaking out?"

"Yeah. I meant that." She blushed as she smiled back.

Then it hit me. This was another time to doubt my sanity.

How could I do this? Lord, how could I go along with this?

Melva hadn't said it outright, but I knew she didn't want anyone knowing about this. Not about the tunnel, not about the still, not about us going there tonight. One never knew who might decide to tell the police and she really wanted to do this for herself.

But …

What if something were to happen? I would be the adult that went into a tunnel with a still in it with two minors and didn't tell anyone else. Oh yeah! That comes off really well. I thought back to how frightened, and yes angry, Jebbin got when I took off on my own to Observatory Park, where the Twombly College Observatory is, without telling anyone after Archie Dawson and Timothy Law were murdered.

An old expression I'd heard my Southern relatives use came to mind. *Sometimes it's better to ask for forgiveness afterward than to seek permission before.* If I just let Jebbin know I was going to be somewhere and would be home late he wouldn't be worryin' about me while I'm playing at being like *Lara Croft: Tomb Raider* in that old video game. Hmm … Emory Crawford: Tunnel Raider. I mentally shook that off and brought my thoughts back to the issue at hand.

And what would it do to Jairus and Amy if something happened to Madison? They weren't the type of parents who hovered and fretted over their children. Their son, Jairus the VII, had been quite the adventurous rascal when he was younger, and even though Madison was their baby, she'd always been into something or other and not always something safe.

And, what about Jairus's own gift of knowing? I realized I hadn't heard from him about any of this, which suddenly seemed strange. Was it on the fritz again?

Even so, could I make the decision to let Madison be involved in this?

On the other hand …

If I told, and Melva were to find out, I would lose her trust and then where would we be? The confession she just made to Madison and me and her willingness to turn herself in impressed me. It showed she was a young lady ready to turn her life around, regaining the confidence she had in herself when she danced onstage and swam in competitions.

It could renew her interest in life, which would make whatever time she had to serve for her crimes go a little easier, I would think. But, I could picture it all draining away if Madison or I didn't honor that trust.

I sighed a mental sigh. At least this way there would be an adult with them. They weren't just running off on their own. They had taken the responsible step. They wanted me there. I simply could not shake the knowin' I had that Melva was the key to finding the answers to all the questions.

Sometimes the past won't stay in the past, and Melva was the bridge.

With a prayer for forgiveness in my heart and fake courage's smile on my face I made my decision.

"Emory?" Melva broke my thoughts.

I'd been thinking longer than I'd realized. "Yeah. Okay," I said none too heartily. "I'll be the wheel man on this job."

We all laughed a little, but it was the nervous laughter of people knowing they were doing something stupid and potentially illegal.

CHAPTER 25

DINNER SUNDAY EVENING WAS INTERESTING.

Jebbin had convinced Deepti that a light meal would be fine since breakfast had been so hearty, and we sat down to enjoy four light vegetarian dishes and a mixed fruit platter. There were Paneer Pinwheels with paneer cheese, green chilies, ginger, and carrot—and maybe some other things as well—rolled into a pastry and sliced into inch-thick pinwheels then baked to perfection. There was Spicy Fried Bhindi, which is basically fried okra, something we're used to eating with Jebbin being from the Missouri Ozarks and my folks being from Georgia. This was Indian style, with thinly sliced tomatoes and wonderful flavorings. There were also things that looked a lot like sausage patties but Deepti said were Veggie Galouti, served on bun-sized paratha flat bread with a yummy dish called Maharashtrian Style Potatoes that featured sweet potatoes and coarsely chopped onions with wonderful spices.

Oh yeah. We were going to be eating well while Deepti was here.

The only thing Jebbin wasn't thrilled with was the fried bhindi dish. It was simply too hot for him.

"This is all just too fantastic, Deepti," he enthused, causing her to blush. "Emory hasn't yet wandered past a basic chicken curry, which she has to keep pretty mild." His mischievous grin graced his lips and his eyes sparkled. "I always say that I like my food bland and my women spicy."

Now I was blushing and everyone else, especially Ragesh, was heartily laughing.

"I take that as a compliment, since I know he means it to be." I said over the laughter. "Although, I'm not sure I'm all that spicy." I added, starting a whole new round of laughter.

"Antonia sent several samples from each of the mummies and we were able to extract DNA from a few of them," Jebbin said during a lull in the conversation.

"Yes!" Chatty lit up. "Jebbin was most helpful with that task while I was working on various tests having to do with the recent unfortunate death. His right hand is wonderfully steady."

"And?" I looked from one man to the other.

"Oh?" Jebbin's eyes had a jolly glint despite the tired dark smudges under them. He probably shouldn't have been at the lab for so many hours straight. "Is there something you want to know about the DNA results, Honey?"

I gave him my what-do-you-think glare, which made him laugh.

"The big news on the Mummies of Sutton House is that … No, that's getting to the good part too quickly. We processed the samples we took from Larry and Melva Suter, since we know they claim to be Sutton descendants. And why would they lie about that? After some really good work on my part, we can now confirm beyond any reasonable doubt that …"

He stopped, eyebrows raised in a 'come on, ask me' look.

I put on my not-too-bright-freshman-college-student voice. "Oh,

Dr. Crawford, please tell us. You confirmed what?"

He grabbed hold of imaginary lapels and threw his chest out theatrically. "We have confirmed that the poor man known to us up until this point as 'Man B' is indeed Mr. Melvin Sutton." Jebbin grinned and lowered his hands. "Since DNA from Man B matches with both Suters, and they both have a reasonable claim to being descendants, it is confirmed as fact."

Oddly, there was no cheering. No burst of relieved enthusiasm. We sat in silence for a few moments.

"I bet they'll be really glad to know what happened to their ancestor," Ragesh said softly. "Even though he was murdered. At least now they know he didn't just run off and abandon his wife and kids."

I pictured Melva and her father in my mind, standing side by side over a new grave in a serene cemetery with gentle smiles on their faces. They could lay Melvin Sutton to rest beside his dear Polly at last.

"They will be, Ragesh. I know they will be."

$\approx$

The dinner conversation moved on to other things. That was a good thing in some regards as my mind was elsewhere, and I would have hated to miss any more pieces of information on either case. Two or three times one or another of my friends at the table had to say my name more than once to get my attention.

The Chatterjees left around 6:30. Deepti told me when we were in the kitchen cleaning up from the meal that she and Chatty realized that Jebbin was tired and were concerned that he would not go to bed if they stayed.

They were right, he wouldn't have.

He announced he was heading for bed as soon as the front door shut behind them. Tony took care of getting him ready since he still needed some help in the bathroom, and I tucked him in at around 7:15. The dear man was snoring before I had even shut the door behind me.

I told Tony I was going to go downstairs to do some work on my computer and might just go to sleep on the sofa in the family room.

"Jebbin is already snoring to beat the band, and he was kind of restless last night, so I think I'll just give us both some space. If he calls you during the night let him know I'm downstairs. He'll understand. It won't be the first time his snoring or covers-stealing has driven me down there."

Tony smiled and laughed. "My Ma used to do the same thing. Thanks for telling me. I'd rather know than have him call me in and the both of us get worried."

I bid him good night and went downstairs. The first step in my late night escapade with the girls completed. The next step was to keep an ear out for when Tony went to bed.

I could sneak out through the sliding doors in the family room and he wouldn't hear me, but I wasn't sure I could get away with "stealing" our car if I left while he was still up. It might not matter too much anyway. Melva wouldn't be able to get out until after Larry got home from closing up The Coal Bin, and she'd said that wouldn't be until after midnight.

My anxiousness was making me antsy.

Our arrangement was that Melva would text "GO" to Madison and me when she was clear. I would drive by Cornelia House to get Madison first since it was just on the other side of the campus, then we'd go get Melva.

But I was going nuts in the house.

I finally gave up around 8:20 and headed for the stairs. I had been hearing Tony in the living room watching TV. Halfway up I remembered that I had wanted to have some innocent place that I could tell Jebbin I had gone to. Now would be the perfect time to do something about that, and Tony wouldn't even ask a bunch of questions about why.

"Tony?"

"Yeah, Emory. You need me for something?"

"No. I just got a text from my friend AnnaMay. She asked if I could come over for a while." I picked up my purse from the back of the dining table chair I always hang it on. My hobo bag was on my shoulder. "She's single and sometimes gets a little lonely at her house at night." I unhooked my keys from the strap as I headed toward the laundry room and the door into the garage. "So I'm heading over there for a while. Don't know how long I'll be, so you don't need to wait up or anything."

"Alright. You have a good time, and say hello to Ms. Langstock for me. I talk to her a couple of times a week when I go to the library to check out books."

"I will, Tony. Goodnight!"

"Goodnight!"

Okay.

I lied.

I don't like to lie but I had to be somewhere other than the house while I waited for the signal.

My laptop and I went to Steak 'n Shake. They are open twenty-four hours. I revisited my teen years by having a chocolate malt and French fries with cheese to dip them in.

I was playing solitaire when someone sat down on the other bench in my booth.

Apparently Jairus's intuition wasn't out of commission. How else could he have found me?

"What is going on tonight, Emory?" No beating about the bush for Jairus Twombly.

"Ah …"

"I know it has to do with the Sutton House, or, at least it has to do with that area, and I know it has to do with Madison, you, and

Melva Suter. What I can't get is any impression about why you're all going out there at night."

"I, ah. We, that is … um."

He stared at me and I stared back.

"You can't tell me." He blinked then looked down at his hands, fingers intertwined, resting on the table. In an absent manner he grabbed a few of the thin fries, dipped them in the cheese sauce, and stuffed them in his mouth.

"Not really, no." I answered while he chewed.

He nodded and swallowed. "Hmm. I guess that makes sense. I've been getting mixed feelings. The only clear one was that I'd find you here right now." He dipped and ate a few more fries. "I haven't had these in ages. Forgot how good they are with the cheese. Is it something dangerous?"

I mulled it over. "Do you mean the fries or what is happening tonight?"

We both chuckled a little. A small, light break in the tension.

"Potentially, but not a surety." I hesitated then added, "At least the girls aren't going on their own. And … and the reason I can't tell you any details is a matter of trust. I, ah … think it would do a great deal of harm if I break this particular trust."

We stared at each other once more until the look in Jairus's eyes softened.

"Then I'll trust you as well. Just tell me, whatever is happening, was it your idea or the girls?"

"Theirs. They invited me and they could have just as easily left me out of it and gone on their own without an adult with them."

"And it's important?"

I nodded firmly. "Yes. It is very important. A life-changing action."

Jairus took some more fries, chewed them slowly then took a deep breath. "Okay. I will steer clear unless I know I have to go out there. I get the least twinge that something's amiss and I'm there, most likely with law enforcement with me."

"I'm all for that, Jairus. I feel better, in fact. I've just had the thought that bringing the police at that point would most likely be a good idea. And I won't tell the girls that we've talked." I paused, then added with a grin, "Though Madison might get a knowin' of her own that her papa might show up."

He smiled his charismatic Twombly smile. "She just might at that. I'll be keeping you all in thought and prayer, Emory."

"Believe me, I am too."

With that, he rose, gave me one more nod, grabbed and dipped a few more fries, and left the restaurant.

Melva's text came in at 12:47.

By 1:10 a.m. we were driving along a county road near Sutton's Lake.

CHAPTER 26

WE PARKED THE CAR ON A FARM IMPLEMENT ACCESS ROAD IN THE cornfield that surrounded the copse of trees and made our way to it under cover of the tall cornstalks. There were probably more trees in the copse now than there had been in 1844. Melvin hadn't made the stand of trees sound very large in his tunnel-diary. Now it was maybe twenty feet long by about ten feet wide.

Scattered clouds were moving in on a southwesterly wind, forerunners of massive clouds to come. Even though the sun had gone down a few hours ago, the air had become muggy and the temperature was going up instead of down. We were supposed to have heavy storms sometime before daybreak, and it felt like it.

Finally, Melva stopped, and the dim light from the small flashlight she carried down by her thigh showed us a door, about three feet square, set flush into the low rise of a hillock. It looked like the entrance to a storm shelter, set into the ground with the far end set about a foot higher than the edge closest to us.

"It had a really old padlock on it that I cut with bolt cutters." Melva's voice nearly blended with the sounds of the wind cutting through the branches of the trees. "I was surprised that the lock hadn't been broken off ages ago."

She used a key hanging on a long chain attached to the belt loop of her jeans to open a shiny new padlock that secured rusty old iron brackets. She grabbed the rope attached to a large iron ring on the right-hand side of the door, tossed the rope over a tree branch, and, using it like a pulley, raised the door until it was nearly vertical. Wrapping the rope around the tree to secure the door, she went back to it and braced it with a small log, released the rope, and then lowered the door flat onto the ground. The door had opened without a sound.

"WD-40." She answered our quizzical looks with a smug smile. "Be careful. It's a long climb down, about sixteen feet or so. The ladder's sturdy. I fixed it all up when I decided to work down there." As if to demonstrate, she lay down on her stomach, swung her feet over the edge, found the rungs with her toes and, using two short ropes she'd strung as handholds, started down the ladder. Madison got onto the ladder next with marvelous agility.

I worked myself into position and started down with considerably less grace. A flat duct, like they put between floor joists for heating and cooling, ran up the left-hand side of the shaft. Melva had indeed put in a vent.

She had turned on a strong battery operated lantern at the bottom of the ladder, which filled the ladder shaft with welcome light. Now she aimed its beam into the tunnel proper. The air was chilly and damp, as one would expect underground. The tunnel appeared to be well built—at least it looked well built to me, but I am no expert on how to build safe tunnels. I reckoned it to be about four feet wide and around six feet high with support beams and lintels about as close together as the studs and joists in a house. I cringed when I noticed that a few of the lintels looked somewhat bowed and some of the support timbers had large cracks in them.

I normally like caves and such, but those saggy and cracked beams were disquieting.

The tunnel ran straight for forty to forty-five feet and then took a sharp turn to the left, as though the Sutton men had started digging off course and had to make a correction. Ten feet on from there, the tunnel shifted again to the left at a gentler angle, so that it was probably running more southeast than due south. I tried to visualize where the house had been before we'd turned down the track into the cornfield. If I was right, we were now heading straight for the house … or at least the farmyard.

After another forty feet or so, the tunnel widened out into what felt like a small room.

And there sat Melva's still. The lantern light made the copper glow warmly, and the gallon-sized glass jugs off to the side sparkled. Up by the ceiling, a double exhaust fan was connected to the vent duct.

"I have no idea what they made this place for." Melva set the lantern down, then waved her arm at the small space. "But it was perfect for the still. If it hadn't gotten bigger I wouldn't have used the tunnel; there wouldn't have been enough room to maneuver."

She moved closer to the still, her eyes shining. Her fingers caressed the copper still proper, the smaller "thump keg", where the alcohol was re-boiled to increase its potency, and then circled round and around the copper "worm"—the tubing where the alcohol vapors from the thump keg condensed and finally dripped into the waiting jug.

"Shame it's caused so much trouble." She looked at it fondly. "I spent so much time cleanin' it up and puttin' it together and then putting in the vent and all. It's the one my dad started with, before he decided to get the permit and make enough to serve in The Coal Bin and had to buy a bigger one. I kinda want to feel proud of it, but it was wrong from the very start. I was stupid to play those f

… dumb machines at the restaurant." She took a deep breath, her eyes on the still. "I was stupid to get in the local games, and I was even more brainless to do something I knew was illegal and think it'd get me outta trouble."

With a firm shake of her head she looked at me.

"That's enough of that." She smacked the rounded shoulder of the still gently. "Let's get this thing taken apart and we can go straight to the cops with it." With a wry grin she added, "I've been there. I know they're open all night."

I thought about that for a moment.

"I don't think you should take it down, Melva." I cautioned. "I think that would be tampering with evidence, for one thing, and I don't really relish us hoisting the pieces out of here with just the three of us."

She stared at the still. "Hmm. Yeah. I get both points. What do you suggest we do?"

"Photos!" Madison chirped as she whipped out her phone and snapped a photo off with a blink of the flash.

All three of us snapped photos of the still from different angles and with or without Melva in them.

"Might as well make it plain that I didn't just pull photos of a still from somewhere else," Melva said as she stood beside it.

"What's down here?"

Neither Melva nor I had noticed Madison moving further down the tunnel to the edge of the lamplight.

"Does it go anywhere?"

"Ah … no. Not really." Melva sounded irritated. "It just sort of stops."

Madison turned. I recognized the look in her eyes. "Let's go see." She grabbed the lantern and started down the tunnel. Melva and I shrugged at each other and followed.

This was by far the longest part of the tunnel, but it ran straight.

We walked along, not saying anything, just looking at all the hard work Melvin Sutton and his three oldest sons had accomplished. Because, of course, it wasn't just digging. They had also carted out the material they were digging through.

"I wonder how they got all the dirt out?" I said aloud to no one in particular.

"I think they hauled it up the shaft," Melva replied. "When I first found the door when I was little, there were some, like, fence posts that had started to rot stuck in the ground at the four corners of the door. I think they had something like a well bucket rigged up."

I nodded. "Makes sense." What a lot of work that had been. I wondered what they were digging for. They hadn't dug all that tunnel just to 'still whiskey!

"Melva?" Madison's voice, just ahead, sounded scared. "There's a hole up there."

"Yep. I think it's an old airshaft. You notice it's not too stuffy back here? It would be if there weren't a way for air to get in. There have been a couple more that you must not have noticed. They still seem to be open at the top, at least you can see some light during the day, but I've never found where they come out since I have no idea where it would be on the top side."

We walked a bit further, and we were almost to the wall at the end, when we felt a shudder.

We heard a shifting.

We saw dust coming from the ceiling.

Just before part of it fell in.

Squatting or kneeling on the floor we huddled together, screaming into each other's ears and covering our heads with our arms until the rush of dirt stopped and only an occasional clink from a few falling pebbles remained.

Once I stopped screaming, a calm came over me. I picked up the lantern, thanking the Lord that it was still with us and still working. I made sure the girls were upright instead of sprawled on the floor bleeding, and then aimed the light at the pile of beams and rubble between the exit and us.

"You two okay?" I panned the light beam back and forth across the debris. The spot of light jiggled and I realized numbly that my hand was shaking.

"Yeah." The quivery reply was in unison.

I focused the light at the top right side of the pile. "There's a small gap there. Can't tell if it goes clear through, but it would be a place to start digging." I turned the light toward the ceiling, like a torchiere lamp, so I could see the girls without shining it in their eyes. "Any volunteers?"

Dirty faces with round owl eyes looked at me.

"We're trapped, aren't we?" Madison whispered. It was a statement, not a question.

"Ah … Um … I ah. I don't know, Madison." And I really didn't, though my mind was yelling at me that we were. "Do you have any ideas, Melva?"

"Tha … that's the … the only way. The only way … ou … out I kn … kn … know of." Melva looked even younger and more frightened than Madison.

My knees were wobbly, my hands clammy and shaky, and sweat was dribbling down the center of my back in a long shuddery line. I figured I looked and felt as bad as they did. I think the only reason I wasn't losing it was that my years of "mom-hood" had kicked in. When something goes wrong, Mom takes charge to protect the children.

And they were both children.

I'd fall apart later.

"Melva, you're a dancer. You have great balance and you aren't much heavier than Madison. I want you to clamber up there and have a look-see. See if that gap is an opening all the way through."

"Y … yeah. I can do that."

I gave her a hand up. "I'll keep the lantern until you are up there and feel balanced well enough to take it."

She nodded and started climbing.

I decided I'd hold off on panicking until after Melva gave her report.

Madison got up to stand by me. I put my arm around her shoulders and she snuggled in closer. Melva took her time, even though it wasn't a very long climb, stopping every time the dirt gave way under her feet. Finally, she reached for the lantern.

"I think it goes through," she said as she took the light from me. "I think I could see some of the ceiling from the light coming through from over here." She held the lantern to the opening.

"Yep! The pile is only about two or three feet thick up here." She looked down at us, her face lit with a joyous smile. "It'll take some work, but we can get out." Melva turned the light on the opposite wall. "It's a good thing, too, as that's the end of Grandpa's dig … What's that?" She was looking over our heads.

Madison and I turned to look behind us. "Where?" we both asked.

"There, about halfway up and toward the left. I'm getting a reflection off something. Some of that dirt musta shaken loose." She added, "I'm sure there didn't used to be that much piled along the bottom edge of the wall."

Madison stepped over to the wall and started looking and feeling around.

"Up a little," Melva coached. "Okay. Now over. No, to the left. Yeah. Further. More."

"Here! You mean here?"

"Yeah. What is it?"

Madison rubbed her fingers back and forth enlarging the shiny spot. Dirt trickled down.

She turned, grinning. "Glass. It's glass. I think we found one of the windows in the house."

CHAPTER 27

MADISON TURNED BACK TO THE WALL TO RUB AWAY MORE OF THE DIRT as Melva and I joined in. Soon, we had uncovered a double hung window and, through the grimy glass, we could see the shadowy inside of a house.

We looked away from the window and at each other.

"It has to be, doesn't it?" Madison voiced what we were all thinking.

Melva cupped her hands against the glass and around her face against the reflection of the lantern and the lit up part of the tunnel behind us. "Oh wow, yeah! It's the main floor of Grandpa's house. You guys weren't there on Friday. You dropped me off and all of us on the team all got our first look at the main floor. We opened one of the windows just enough to scrape a few soil samples off the packed dirt but not let all the dirt fall into the house. I think this is that window. That might be why the dirt gave way so easily when the ceiling fell in. We'd already disturbed it." She looked over at us. "I don't think any of us woulda guessed in a million years that there was a tunnel on the other side of that dirt."

For a while we all stood, hands cupped around our faces, staring into the Sutton House. I felt a shiver run through Melva and heard Madison whisper a "Wow!" It was an even stranger feeling than the one I'd had the first time I went through the house's roof and down the ladder into a bedroom. Altogether too weird to be nearly twenty feet underground and looking through a window into someone's living room. I thought of those archeologists who have excavated the cities under cities in London and Chicago and other places. Whole neighborhoods had been covered so that new buildings could be built over them, and now they were being dug back out, still underground, for scholars to study and tourists to visit. I'd seen photos that were exactly like what we were looking at right now.

I stood up and stretched my back. "I vote we open the window and go out through the house instead of trying to dig through the debris. I know they leave the ladder in place since the place is guarded."

"Ah, yeah. Guarded." Melva huffed. "Like I need more trouble with the cops for somehow coming out of a house no one is supposed to be in."

Madison and I looked at her.

"Well, I *would* be in more trouble." She put her fists on her hips. "They said I better watch it 'cause they'd be keeping an eye on me." She paused, and then drew herself up to stand straighter. "I want to turn myself in on my own, not be caught doing something else."

We all just stood there for a few moments.

"Good point, Melva," I said as I looked at the window once more. "We aren't supposed to be here at all and it would raise the question of how we got in here to begin with. I suggest that we see what we find when we get up there. The guard isn't walking the perimeter or anything. He's parked where he can see up and down the road and the full east side and north sides of the pavilion, but I bet we could get a look at him and his SUV without him seeing us just because he isn't expecting anyone to already be inside the pavilion. It may turn out he won't be a problem."

Melva nodded thoughtfully. "Okay." She finally said.

Madison agreed and we opened the window, which wasn't easy to do with all the dirt that had sifted into the frame, but it finally rose enough that we could squeeze through. We climbed into the house. At the foot of the stairs we shut off the lantern and used cellphone light to help us see as we climbed.

We went into the master bedroom where the ladder was.

I stared at the place where Melvin and Reginald had died. "I do have something I wanted to tell you guys, something I found out going through old papers and stuff with AnnaMay at the library."

"What?" Melva asked.

"I think they told you and your dad that Man B was Melvin Sutton, didn't they?"

"Yeah. They did. Figured it out from DNA they got from Dad and me and ... the two, you know. The bodies. When all this other stuff is behind us we're going to make sure he's buried next to Polly."

I smiled at her. "I had the feeling you two would do that." I paused. "I know who the other man was."

"Really?" Melva asked.

"Wow." Madison sounded impressed.

"Are you gonna tell us or make us wait?" Melva sounded irritated. It had been a long, exhausting night.

"I'm telling you now. His name was Reginald Leander Westford, R.L.W., and he was the son of the man who was the next richest man in Golden County after Jairus Twombly the First."

"I've heard about the Westfords," Madison chirped. "Something went wrong with their family. I never learned what, but they ended up selling their mansion and leaving the county. The house is still there and a surgeon who works at one of the big hospitals in Springfield lives in it now."

"Guess that's why there aren't any of them still around, like your family is." Melva's voice sounded taut, strained. Like she wasn't being honest with us. "The diaries had an R.L. and an R. person in them. Didn't Polly say he owned the land and that he was the one they sharecropped for? That might be why he was in the house." Her tone was now sharp, edgy.

"It probably was, Melva," I agreed. "Remember, Polly was wondering if he might be getting upset with Melvin."

We all went silent. I got that "rabbit ran over my grave" chilly shiver up my back, and I knew there was something more. Something Melva knew relating to nowadays but wasn't saying. Something that was upsetting her and that, perhaps, should bother me too but it stayed in the shadows at the back of my mind.

With the cellphones shut off and in our pockets, we eased quietly up the ladder.

Madison had only gone up a couple of rungs when she said, "Sounds like it's pouring rain up here."

"Possible," Melva said as she took hold of the ladder, "but it always sounds heavy hitting that plastic."

Madison had been right. The predicted storms had come with a vengeance.

Moving to the east side of the enclosure, Melva eased open a slit where the eastern plastic wall met the north facing wall and all three of us peered out. It was country dark. We could see the glow of Twombly's street and business lights reflecting off the clouds and rain to the east, but where we were we could barely see a thing until some lightning flashed.

To the east and slightly north, we saw the guard's SUV. We waited. FLASH!

We saw him, head tipped back, obviously asleep where it was dry and cozy.

I smiled. "I think we're clear to go, ladies. There's a spot not too far to the west of here where there's a way to cross over the drainage ditch. I think we should head for that. The pavilion will block his view for most of our way, *if* he wakes up, and after that I think we'll have cover from high grass and scrub bushes."

The girls agreed, so we crawled out under the western flap. We crouched as we ran across the shore of Sutton's Lake and across the road out of Twombly by the light of a cellphone held low to the ground. Down into the low ditch on the far side of the road, through the foot of water in it, and up out of the ditch. The girls had to help me out; I kept slipping. We went two rows of corn deep into the field to hide the light from our phones and walked parallel to the road. It was a struggle for me, out of shape as I am. I knew I'd be aching tomorrow.

We walked at a slower pace the rest of the way to my car. I took the girls home, went into my house through the laundry room and straight into the main bathroom. I stared at the dust-gray face that stared back at me, ghost-like, from the mirror. There was no way I was sleeping in our bed or on the sofa without taking a shower.

Chapter 28

THE RAIN CONTINUED TO FALL. LIGHTER NOW. STRAIGHT-DOWN RAIN without the usual prairie winds blowing it sideways.

Large noisy drops off the eaves mixed with more constant lighter drops and drummed on the roof of our screened-in porch where I sat sipping my second mug of Aine's Realignment Tea and listened to the music of the predawn rain. The moist air was refreshing, not muggy, with enough of yesterday's cool temperatures remaining to keep it pleasant. Aine had told me to drink Realignment when I had time for solitude. I had taken a shower and was wide awake now, with only an hour and a half before I had to start my day, so it seemed silly to try to go to sleep. The early morning hour was calming, the sound of the rain soothing, so I figured the time was ripe for quiet contemplation.

I wasn't sure what the tea was supposed to realign, nor was I sure it would do much good with a tired out brain, but I figured it couldn't hurt anything. Then again, I'd thought the Discernment Tea couldn't hurt anything either and had gotten more strange results than I'd bargained for.

Nothing overpowering happened when I'd brought out Melvin Sutton's tunnel diary as I drank my first mugful of Realignment and thumbed through it. Mostly, it was boring. It recorded how many feet they dug each time they worked. It described putting in the small airshafts. They'd toted the dirt away in wheelbarrows and spread it on the surrounding fields, or took it all the way to Sandy Ford where the road into Twombly crossed Okaw Creek. Obviously, they did what needed to be done to keep the project secret.

I also found out what the tunnel was for.

Coal.

Reginald thought there was coal under his land.

This was not completely unreasonable, as there had been a good deal of coal in the area back in that day and there was still a large active mine in the southern part of the county. Once there had been mines throughout Golden County and many people today carried subsidence insurance just in case their land was over an old mine.

Someone had given Reginald the idea there was coal under that section of lowland along the west side of Okaw Creek, but I couldn't find out who it was. Chances were that Melvin didn't know who it was either—only that Reginald had alluded to someone telling him there was coal there. The diary had comments from Melvin like, "I sure hope that fella knew what he was talking about," and "We found nary an outcropping as that fella said he had seen, and we ain't even hit no brown coal as would be expected as shallow as we are lookin'."

I closed the diary. It was almost 4:00 a.m. I drained the last of my second mug of tea and stood up to go back into the house when the lightning bolt hit me.

The mental kind of lightning, that is.

Realignment Tea indeed. I could feel bits of memories coming together and dropping into place like pieces of a jigsaw puzzle.

I knew where I'd heard the name Westford before AnnaMay helped me discover who R.L.W. was.

I ran into the house, booted up my laptop, and found the email Madison had sent with the transcript of the conversation she'd listened in on between her father and the family lawyer, Simone Bogardus.

And there it was.

The officer questioning Melva had asked if she knew someone named Peter Westford.

And she had.

Melva had told Madison and me that Pete ran the gambling, Pete ran the parties, but she had never used his full name when talking to us.

Time intertwines. Future harkens back. Past foreshadows future.

A Westford, Reginald Leander Westford, forced Melvin Sutton into digging for coal in 1844.

A Westford, Peter Westford, forced Melva Suter-Sutton into making illegal moonshine in the present.

Sometimes the past won't stay in the past.

CHAPTER 29

I WENT THROUGH MY MORNING ROUTINE ON AUTOPILOT. I SAID GOOD morning to Jebbin and Tony before they headed off to do Jebbin's morning physical therapy. I greeted Deepti and Ragesh when they arrived, grocery bags full of ingredients for dinner in their arms, but didn't even think to ask what she had planned.

I thought of telling our friend, Detective Jason Anderson of the Twombly Police Department. Unlike Henry Schneider, Jason could be trusted to handle the information with some tact. And, since Peter Westford distributed gambling machines inside Twombly city limits *and* Melva lived in Twombly proper, it could be his jurisdiction, unlike the drinking parties and, most likely, the gambling that wasn't on the machines. They were all out of town under the jurisdiction of the Golden County Sheriff's Department.

Another conundrum.

I seemed to be piling one on top of the other. As far as I knew, no one knew about Melva, Madison, and me being out around

Sutton's Lake last night. I not only knew who the other mummy was, I knew that he had been having his sharecropper dig for coal, and I knew his family had lied about his going missing. I also knew a Westford descendant was definitely behind the illegal gambling and boozing in the present.

That was a lot to keep to myself.

"Emory?"

Deepti's concerned tone and my name caught my attention.

"Hmm? What?" I turned away from the sliding glass door.

She smiled. "You are not all here this morning, I think. Are you wanting some breakfast before you leave for the dig?"

She had no idea how right she was about my not being all here.

"No, thank you, Deepti. I'll just …"

My text alert sounded.

"I'll just head over to the dig now and get something at Casey's on the way." I paused and read the text. "Oops. Actually, breakfast sounds great." I looked at my friend and laughed at her confused look. I waggled my phone. "The text was from Dr. Koerner. The rain is supposed to stop around eight or nine. He wants to let the area dry out a bit so we'll be starting today at one-thirty. You've got me for breakfast and lunch too."

Deepti laughed and clapped her hands once. "We will not be stuck, nor will you miss being at the dig this very rainy morning."

"We can work on fiddling!" Ragesh stuck his head in the door. "I claim Auntie Emory for fiddling. Fiddling! Fiddling!" He cheered as he danced about, pumping his fist.

"You will share Auntie Emory, Ragesh." His mother's voice was calmly strong, a voice not to be trifled with.

My text alert sounded again.

"Yes, Mother," Ragesh replied as I checked my message. He sulked for a few seconds before brightening up again. "May I have her first, Mom?"

"Yes, you may." Deepti's voice was melodious again. "You may do fiddling for one hour after breakfast, then it will be my turn to have time with my friend."

I saw her turn toward me out of the corner of my eye.

"I want to ask about the stitchery picture on the floor stand downstairs," she continued, "and then we can chatter while we prepare lunch."

"That sounds … ah." I looked away from the message. "Sorry, Deepti. Fiddle time with Ragesh and stitchery time with you sounds wonderful. I need to look over this message then I'll come in and help with breakfast."

I walked into the living room and looked at my phone.

The message was from Melva.

OMG! Text from Dr. K. reminded me—I forgot the evidence! I have to go back tonight! We have to! I'll text Madison. Will use same setup we used last night. I'll text GO! Be ready. Sorry to make us go back. ☹ Will see you at dig this aft.

I had forgotten all about it too. There was nothing for it really. She needed to have the solid evidence of that video; otherwise it would be just her word against Peter's as to who controlled the moonshine operation.

After breakfast, Ragesh and I headed downstairs to the family room with our instruments in hand.

We worked on his playing by ear again first. I had given him the exercise of playing "Twinkle, Twinkle, Little Star". He was to work on humming it and then to begin to find the notes, no sheet music allowed, on his violin. Ragesh refused to call it a fiddle yet; he said it wouldn't be a fiddle until he could play a bluegrass song on it. As I expected, he moved the tune from his mind, to vocalization, to his instrument with no problems. He played it flawlessly.

After playing the song a couple of times through together, I used it to begin teaching him the Nashville, or *simple*, shuffle. It's one of the most common bowing patterns in bluegrass fiddling, and it gives any song that bluegrass feel.

Our hour flew by and then Deepti came downstairs. Ragesh went upstairs to practice a little more and then play games on his iPad while I told his mother about the craft of needlepoint.

"And this picture?" She gestured across the surface of my stitchery of Katsushika Hokusai's print "The Great Wave off Kanagawa". "Why did you choose it?"

"I don't really know, other than I've always liked it, and when I saw the canvas I was drawn to it. That was well before all the flooding this year. It seems almost prophetic now." I brushed my fingers over my even stitches.

"Yes, it has been a time drawn to water." Her tone was distant yet soothing. "And the past as well, has it not?"

"It has." I picked up the card that had come with the canvas. "Your saying that has made me wonder." I took a moment to read. "It says this print was drawn in the early 1830s and is one of a series of wood block prints that all have Mt. Fuji in them. None has the emotional pull across cultures that this picture does." I looked at Deepti and grinned. "Which is probably why this one is the most famous of them all. Most people don't even know about the others." My eyes went back to the date on the card and a chill swept through me. "Not all that long before the flood took the Sutton House." I muttered.

"Hmm." Her tone was hypnotic, like the music of a snake charmer. "A convergence of times, like the convergence of the creeks that helped cause that big surge—as Jebbin explained to Nibodh." She nodded. "It is the way of time."

The sound of the rain outside dropping into puddles and pouring through the downspouts added to the somber moment.

~

The guys came in for lunch, all smiles.

"Have we got news for you, Hon!" Jebbin crowed. I'm sure he would have swung me round like a square dancer if he'd been on two good legs.

"You didn't walk all the way across campus, did you?" I scowled at him.

The excited glow on his face faded a bit.

"What? Oh! My pirate gear." He looked down and patted the strap around the top of his thigh. His glow returned, along with his smile. "No. I didn't walk all the way home. But I did wear it off and on at the lab and I walked up our sidewalk and front steps. Tony said the porch stairs are good for me since they've got a wide tread and a fairly low rise. He says they'll help build up my legs. But who cares about that?" He waved the conversation aside. "We know which man in the house did the shooting."

"Wow!" I looked at Jebbin then at Chatty. "And you haven't said a thing," I said to the latter.

"It is being very difficult." Chatty beamed at me. "But I told Jebbin he could have the honor, seeing as he did the work."

"And I," Jebbin cut in, "won't say any more until we are seated at the table and enjoying our lunch."

Even though I reckoned I already knew who the shooter had been, I kept quiet and joined everyone else as we hurried to get lunch on the table and all of us seated.

"Okay, Uncle Jebbin." Ragesh jumped right in. "Spill."

We all laughed as the lad stuffed a forkful of salad into his mouth.

"Well, you all remember that we found fingerprints on the brass powder flask?"

We all nodded, our mouths full of crunchy salad.

"And that we rehydrated the fingertips of the mummies? We got really good sets of prints from both of them. After that, it really wasn't too hard to match them up."

"No, not difficult," Chatty put in after swallowing. "We, of course, scanned everything into the computer."

"And we proved beyond any doubt that our shooter was Man A." Jebbin beamed. "The only letdown to it all is that we can't plug them into any of the fingerprint bases and get his name. But his *are* the only prints on the flask, so he was the only one who used it to load the gun."

"Wow, again!" I cheered. "And since you know that the other man is Melvin Sutton, that clears his name for the family."

The conversation went on, but my mind didn't follow it. I knew the man's name and even a good deal of his background. And once again, I felt bad. I should have shared my information with my dear man. I had the watch from the scene and photocopies of Westford family papers that proved he was Reginald Leander Westford. But, if the name Westford got mentioned, the house of cards Madison and I had built to protect to Melva until she could face everything on her own would collapse. Oh, Lord, I prayed in my heart, let the guys be understanding about what we've done, or Melva might not be the only one in jail.

I was getting anxious about my new plans for tonight and for all of it to be over. But I still had this afternoon to get through.

CHAPTER 30

THE AFTERNOON AT THE DIG WAS ACTUALLY RATHER DULL. WE WERE doing the less exciting ... well, at least less exciting to those of us not pursuing a career in archeology ... work of recording data. How the house itself was constructed. How the furniture was constructed. What sorts of fabrics were used in the large oval braided rug on the floor in what appeared to have been the living room area of the main floor's open layout, and in the smaller hooked rugs in the bedrooms.

I caught Melva and Madison looking toward the window on the main floor that had been our escape route from the tunnel more than once. But all was well. You couldn't tell from a cursory glance that there wasn't a wall of dirt behind it—why would it show? Unless someone shone a light directly into it, it looked just as dark as the others. And so the afternoon went by without incident for the three of us. Neither did we talk to each other very much. Everyone was busy taking notes, and it would have attracted attention if the three of us had huddled together.

The only really interesting piece of information was that Twombly College had decided they were going to take steps to preserve the house. Most likely, it would be disassembled piece by piece and reassembled on the surface. Ceek said a location at the top of the rise to the west was being considered, since it could not be legally put up on the flood plain, where it had originally stood.

I couldn't face going home for dinner and needing to work so hard at not tipping my hand about the tunnel and Melva's plans.

I called Deepti, made my apologies, and said Nancy Walker and Oscar Hornsby from the dig had invited me to have dinner with them and that we wanted to discuss things we'd found at the house as well as the College's plans for the house itself. She was disappointed, I could tell, but not upset. We both have husbands who work for law enforcement; we're used to interrupted plans.

Dinner was me alone at Gulotta's. Juliano, the owner, let me order a child's portion of lasagna and a glass of red wine. That and a small salad from the salad bar was more than enough. I wanted the wine to help me calm down, and I didn't want a big meal in my stomach. The rest of the evening I spent at Steak 'n Shake, like before.

The text came from Melva at 12:50 a.m.

"Melva?" I got her attention as we neared the farm lane into the cornfield.

"Yeah?" came her distracted reply. I was sure she was focused on getting the evidence then going to the police.

"I want you to know I believe in you. I know you're going to do what you've promised and that you're going to straighten your life out if you can handle this the way you need to."

"Thanks, Emory." She sounded relieved. "Thanks."

I turned off the headlights and turned into the lane, drove down about as far as the night before, and stopped. I turned around to look at Melva.

"And I think a lot of other folks will stand by you as well when all is said and done. You won't be alone. So let's just get down there, get the little tackle box, and get this all over with. We all good to go?"

"Yeah," both girls replied in unison. We left the Beetle and started walking to the tunnel.

⁀

We weren't being all that quiet down in the tunnel, and for some reason, we weren't worried about the fact that we hadn't gone back to shut and lock the door at the entrance the night before.

"This'll be a quick trip." Melva reminded us. "If we can get to the still, I know right where the tackle box is. I'll grab it and we get out."

We walked along quickly, keeping a close eye on the ceiling for any signs that it was weaker than before.

Everything looked good around the first curve, but Melva went stiff and paused.

"Can ya feel it?" she whispered. "Can ya smell it?"

When we didn't answer she answered her own questions.

"The still is running and it's running hot."

We ran around the second, more obtuse curve, and down to where the little room opened out. There sat the still, the propane burner's flame burning high against the bottom of the boiler. We crossed the threshold into the room and stopped.

"What the hell?" Melva was furious … and scared. We all were scared.

And that's when a man stood up from behind the still and leveled a pistol at us.

We froze—bodies and voices, and then Melva wheezed out a name.

"Pete."

"Yeah, Melva. Who'd you expect? Maybe the little Twombly Tart's daddy or maybe the old lady's husband?" Peter Westford looked me up and down. "Nah, couldn't be him, he's hobblin' around like one of them old pirate dudes."

Melva had regained herself and now seemed amazingly unfazed. Perhaps because she'd dealt with him before? She scowled at him. "How'd you find this tunnel?"

"Followed you all last night." Pete smirked. "Should'a followed you all the way down but figured you'd bring whatever you had stashed down here back up with ya, so I didn't. Then I felt the ground shake. Figured you was all buried just like your however-many-greats grandpa, so I just left. Found out this afternoon that you'd popped back up like a clingy whore. So I watched your house again, saw which way you were heading, and here we are. Just made sure I got here first so I could surprise you—or should I say I got *back* here. I'd checked it out earlier this evening and thought I'd make ya one last batch of shine."

I've never seen such a cold, empty smile.

"Surprise!" He almost purred the word. "Surprise, you rotten little Sutton. The way my family tells it, Old Melvin had pulled some scam on my great-whatever-grandpa and it was all your family's fault that he had to be sent to Quincy. He died on his way there, so we figure Old Melvin murdered him. It never mattered much to me. Couldn't see much sense in carin' 'bout the past like that. But now? Yeah, don't the whole town know now that not only is the house and the original loser still around but so are his filthy brats. More rotten Suttons around to cause us Westfords trouble. 'Cept not much longer. So sad, too bad," he sing-songed. "You and your best friends here are going to disappear just like he did."

Peter started edging out from behind the still, the gun still trained on us. I caught a brief look of surprise, as if he'd expected us to move away from him to our left and closer to the over-hot still as he moved closer to us from our right. But we didn't. Especially Melva, who didn't seem nearly as petrified as Madison and I.

He was across from us, standing in the middle of the opening to the part of the tunnel that led to the house, his back to the open empty space, when he stopped.

"Move!" he shouted. "Get over by the still, bitches."

Madison, who was closest to the still, moved half a step to her left. But no more.

I was in the middle and hadn't decided if I was going to move or not.

Melva, oddly enough, had moved a step to her right. She drew in a sharp breath and almost smiled. I reckoned she had more to say.

"Do you know who shot Tom?"

My God! A cop in an interrogation room couldn't have sounded any more in charge than she did.

"What busi …"

"You're gonna kill me, I wanna know. Simple as that. I wanna know."

Pete chuckled, then smirked again. The unpleasant expression seemed to be one he used a lot.

"Me. I shot the f …ing little university boy who thought he was so much better than me, even though he owed me more than his daddy makes in a year. A reliable source—and I got a lotta them in this county—told me the little fart was gonna rat me out to the cops since he couldn't pay up. So …"

He smiled his unsmile again.

"I knew you were drunk. I knew he was stoned. I had some of my helpers hand two idiots the pistols, not the sort of thing I'd do myself." He huffed a laugh. "My helpers told the idiots to hand 'em to the two jerks who were pissed at each other and pointed them at you and Tommy Boy."

He laughed heartily. It had more feeling than his smile but was just as evil. Maniacal.

Peter went on with his tale. "I started yellin' 'Duel! Duel!' And all the little stoners and drunks started yellin' it, too, and you two little nothin's took the pistols, did what you'd been told to do and ... BOOM! You shot the ground, which was a riot, by the way. BOOM! Little University Fart shot your leg. BOOM! I was standing behind you and shot the little fart while you were shaking your damn gun at him. End of story." Peter closed his eyes, obviously reliving the moment with pleasure.

He should have been living this moment instead, because a rifle barrel slowly appeared between Melva and me.

I don't think Melva saw it, she was so focused on Peter, but I did. Madison did, too, and nudged my left arm.

Peter opened his eyes. Then he *really* opened his eyes.

"What the ..."

"Shut up, Westford. Just shut up."

All I could see was the rifle.

Melva knew the voice. "Dad?"

The girl was amazing. Even though her voice now shook, she didn't even turn to look, which might have given Peter a distraction he could have used.

"Yeah."

With a grace like I'd seen in his daughter, the dancer, Larry Suter slid into the room and in front of us in one move.

"You all get out of here," Larry ordered.

"But, Dad ..."

"Now ..."

"I'll shoot the still!" Peter screamed. "They move, I'll make it blow!"

"And bury yourself? I don't think so. You ain't got it in you to do that, and you ain't getting out of here without getting past me, and I ain't moving. Girls, get out of here."

We took off running. We got to the end of the slant-wise tunnel and took the soft curve.

Jairus Twombly was there waving us on. "Go! Go!"

We went.
We got to the tighter curve.
And past.
Almost, I was thinking, to the ladder.
Then came the blast.

CHAPTER 31

I WAS ON THE FLOOR. DUST DRIZZLING DOWN ON MY HEAD. THE occasional clink of something small falling.

I wasn't sure what day it was. Was it Sunday? Hadn't something like this happened on Sunday night?

"Daddy!"

"Papa!"

Primal. Desperate.

I heard shuffling noises all around me.

That didn't happen on Sunday. Sunday was just Madison, Melva, and me in the tunnel and we went through the Sutton House.

Why was I still in the tunnel?

"Ma'am?"

Someone with a man's voice took hold of my shoulder.

"Can you hear me, ma'am?"

I opened my eyes. I was still in the tunnel and where we were still had a ceiling. I could see it behind the face looking down at me. Who knew what the rest of the tunnel was like?

I wished I didn't feel so hazy. "Can I hear you? Yes. Yes, I can. Where ... where are the girls?"

"They, ah, ran on back down the tunnel and they should have stayed put. But I, ah, think their fathers are back down there. Some of the other EMTs have headed down there after them. I'm going to take care of you. I'm going shine a little light in your eyes now. You know, check your pupils. Okay. Do you hurt badly anywhere in particular, ma'am?"

"Ah ..." I took a few moments to assess myself as well as I could. "My head. And my knees."

"Okay, ma'am, I'll get those checked out here."

He started checking me out for bumps, bruises, and ...

I didn't want to think about breaks.

"Call me Emory."

"Hmm?" he sort of responded.

"Instead of ma'am. I'm Emory Crawford. Husband teaches at Twombly College."

He spoke to his radio instead of me. "I've got a middle-aged female with trauma to the right rear of her head, possible involvement of both parietal and occipital areas. Abrasions to the scalp that are bleeding. Also jeans torn on both knees with resulting abrasions, and bruising to both knees. Initial exam doesn't show any other areas of bleeding."

"Board and stabilize her. One of the men will be coming out first."

"Will do. Out." He looked at me. "I thought you looked a little familiar to me, Mrs. Crawford. I'm Bruce. I graduated from Twombly College and took my chemistry classes from Dr. Crawford. You just relax as best you can. I'm going to put in an I.V. to get you some fluids and a bit of something to help with pain. Got to be careful, though, because you do have a head injury. Want you staying awake for me if you can."

"Okay, Bruce. I'll do my best."

He called someone else over and they moved me onto a board and lightly strapped me in, then Bruce got busy putting in my I.V. Just as he finished, other EMTs came through carrying someone else who was strapped to a board.

Melva trudged along on the far side of the board from me. She didn't look good at all. Her shoulders sagged, her head hung down. I could see that one of her arms was up as it would be if she was holding Larry's hand.

"Melva?"

"Emory!" Unexpectedly she came over and gave me as much of a one-armed hug as she could with me strapped to a board. "He's hurt pretty badly." She sniffed deeply, working hard at not crying long enough to talk to me. "They, ah … won't tell me much. Keep saying it's … it's too early to, ah, tell. He's unconscious." A softness filled her eyes. "He came for me, Emory. He came for us. I've been so … (sniff) … stupid. I just hope there'll be some way …" She sniffed again and dragged her filthy sleeve across her drippy nose. "Some way I can show him how sorry I am."

Melva held out something for me to see. An olive-green oblong metal tackle box.

"I got the proof." It brought a little smile to her lips. "They'll know it wasn't my dad making the shine for the parties. They'll know Pete made me make it for him."

She looked over at her father and tucked the box back under her jacket between her right arm and her side.

"I think they're hooking up the board so they can get him out of here. I gotta go. Madison's dad isn't hurt too bad. Looks like she and me got the least of it."

She suddenly noticed the bandaging on my head and the I.V. bag.

"Oh no! You're hurt! I'm so sorry. I …" Melva looked as the head of the board her dad was on started to rise. To my surprise, she lightly kissed my forehead then stood up. "I gotta go. I'll come visit you." She called back over her shoulder.

There was a noise like a lawnmower coming down the entry shaft and the board with Larry Suter on it rose. As soon as they had Larry up top and Melva had headed up the ladder, another board came into view with Madison walking alongside. It had to be Jairus.

She looked over at me, tear tracks white through the dust coating her face.

"Papa's okay, Emory." Her voice was shaky and sounded like a little girl's. "Hurt his ankle so they don't want him trying to climb out of here. That's why he's on the board." Her eyes showed her worry and she was holding fast to her Papa's right hand.

Jairus's head lifted and he looked at me. He had a nasal cannula in his nose.

"I'm fine, Emory." He smiled and pointed to his nose. "They think I got a bit too much dust is all." He explained. "I'll see you up top."

A few moments later the lawnmower sounds and Jairus on his board slowly ascended out of the tunnel. Madison climbed up shortly after.

As my board and I cleared the opening into the tunnel I heard someone yelling.

It was Sergeant Henry Schneider. He had grabbed Melva by her right arm and was yanking the tackle box away from Melva.

"What's this? Huh, kid? You sneaking some of that moonshine outta there? Just had to have another swig of it?" He popped open the lid. "Photos and a memory card?" He shook her. "What? You stealing stuff from people to blackmail them or something?"

"No!" Melva was screaming back. "Let me go! They're taking my dad. I gotta go be with my dad."

Henry dropped the box and wrenched Melva's arm around behind her back as he pulled his cuffs off his belt. The card and the photos spilled on the wet ground as he snapped the cuffs closed.

"Dad!" Melva strained to get to her father.

"He can't hear you anyway, kid. We've been watchin' you just like I said we would and you're into all this up to your neck and past. You ain't goin' nowhere but back to jail."

As Henry dragged her off I saw Twombly Police Detective Jason Anderson, our friend and a levelheaded, fair officer, gather up the old tackle box and its contents then head toward the road where all the various law enforcement vehicles were parked.

I started crying.

Not at all what poor Melva had hoped for and none of us who cared most for her had been able to stand up for her. I felt horrible. The only good thing was Jason quietly picking up that box. I smiled through my tears. He'd make sure that evidence was handled properly.

Larry Suter had been put into a helicopter, which lifted up then headed south to one of the large hospitals in Springfield. Jairus and I were loaded into ambulances and headed off east toward Twombly.

It was all over.

⌒

Madison stopped by later to tell me she and her papa were heading home. Jairus had sprained—or strained—his ankle while running. Other than that he was well enough to be home.

"He had me call Mama before I came inside the hospital," my young friend went on, "and tell her to call Mrs. Bogardus before she headed over to the hospital. I'm sure she'll be reporting Sergeant Schneider's treatment of Melva, and she'll keep her away from him too if she can at all. I sure felt bad about that. Melva could have at least been allowed to go to the hospital with an officer or something."

"We'd like to think so, but she is a criminal and the authorities often see that first and not much else." My voice held my sadness over the situation. "I'm sure Simone Bogardus will manage to arrange for her to visit him in the hospital as soon as she can."

"Yep. She's really good." Then Madison frowned. "I shouldn't stay. The doctor was just giving Mama some last little instructions about taking care of Papa, and you need your rest too. I'm glad your head wasn't hurt too badly."

"Me too. No fracture or concussion. Just a really bad scrape." My hand went up to touch my new bald patch. "Chatty will be coming to pick me up soon. I'm going to have some trouble getting around for a few days with my banged up knees, but at least there are plenty of helpers at our house right now."

Just then the television in my little ER cubicle beeped for a special announcement from our local station. The new picture was of local newscaster Dave Collier, standing under an umbrella an aide was holding over him.

"We're on the scene in the early morning gloom and rain a few miles west of Twombly. As you can see a huge swath of the flood plain and surrounding farm fields are under what amounts to a swift flowing river of water. John," Dave said to his cameraman, "I want the shot off me and down the road to the west. Right, that's got it. The heavy rains of Sunday and the continuous rains of Monday, both in our area and northeast of us, have resulted in an immense flash flood that hit the area about half an hour ago. As you can see, County Road 1550 is completely under water just about fifty yards away from where we're standing. The entire area of the recent excavation by Twombly College where they found the long lost Sutton House is now under about eight feet of water, which is still rising. There had been talk about dismantling the house, reassembling it, and making a museum out of it. Back on me, John."

Our view slowly panned back.

"Thanks. I think I can confidently say that plan will not be happening. There was an open hole through the roof of the buried house and I'm certain that it is now completely flooded. And," he looked around then back at the camera, "the water is getting closer and we need to be getting out of here. This is Dave Collier reporting from the massive flooding of Okaw and Rock Creeks west of Twombly."

Madison and I looked at each other. I wondered if I looked as blanched as she did.

"We could have all been in the tunnel or up top after the rescue," she whispered while shaking her head.

"Yeah. We could have." I sounded raspy and breathless, like a long-time smoker. "Us and all the rescue people and cops. We all could have been washed away."

Madison turned away. "I need my folks. I'll … I'll see you later, Emory."

"Bye, Hon," I said to her back as she dashed out of my curtained cubicle. I reached for the phone on the small bedside table. I needed to let Chatty know to get here as soon as he could. I wanted to be home with my husband and friends.

CHAPTER 32

WITHIN THE NEXT FEW WEEKS A LOT HAPPENED TO DRAW EVERYTHING to a conclusion—and yet it didn't either.

Since Melva confessed to making and distributing distilled alcohol—moonshine—without a permit, underage drinking, and participating in illegal gambling she didn't need to go through a full trial. She was sentenced to one year in Decatur Correctional Center, a minimum-security facility for women. Plus, she was assessed the full fine of $25,000.

It eventually became common knowledge that Larry Suter's spinal cord was damaged. He had ended up half buried in the cave-in … the last to run from where the still was. He was hailed as a hero, having kept Peter Westford distracted so the rest of us had more time to escape.

And Twombly College had planned to reconstruct the house, and maybe do something to develop the area into an historical park. But, of course, the house was well and truly gone now.

It wasn't quite what any of us had hoped for.

But a year can bring a lot of changes.

⁓

"Sit, Persey. Alright, good boy. There you go. Go find Sophie." At a hand signal from Melva, the medium-sized service dog, Persey, being short for Perseverance, lunged into the dog run at the Furever Friends Garden, then Melva, Larry, and Georgia made their way over to where the rest of us were sitting at a couple of picnic tables inside the garden proper.

It was a private one-year anniversary potluck picnic celebration for those of us who had been intimately involved with both the old and new events that happened at Sutton's Lake.

Jebbin and I brought my ham and pasta salad, various kinds of chips, hotdogs, and our portable grill. The Twomblys, Jairus, Amy, and Madison, brought eye of round steaks, their chef's out-of-this-world potato salad and homemade buns for the steak sandwiches and the hotdogs and all the condiments anyone could wish for. The Suttons … oh, yes! Larry and Melva officially changed their name to Sutton, along with that of the newest member of the family, Georgia. The manager of The Coal Bin was now also wife, step-mom, and a beloved part of the family. They brought all the beverages and one of the new, and popular, additions to the restaurant's menu, Melva's own "Stir-Slaw".

AnnaMay Langstock provided Grasshopper, French Silk, and Banana Cream pies, which were being kept in a cooler, for dessert.

No, she hadn't been involved like the rest of us had. She hadn't fallen through any roofs nor been caught in any cave-ins, but she had informed me that, "You want me there, Library Minion Crawford. The Wizardess of the Library has info you all want to hear."

No one minded.

"So," Jairus started a new conversation as we dug into our slices of pie. "What did you all think of the grand opening yesterday? Did we do it up right and proper?"

"It was so cool!" Madison smiled at her papa.

Melva glanced heavenward at Madison's usual enthusiasm. "Official cheerleader for the Twombly Appreciation Society."

Madison threw her a shocked look then they both laughed.

"It was really great, Mr. Twombly," Melva added, and the rest of us agreed.

"I was so glad we got everything done in time," Jairus went on. "I wanted to make sure it was ready for when you'd be released, Melva. It was all intended as a bit of a welcome home for you, at least by me, as well as opening the historic site and the bird sanctuary."

"Thanks, Mr. Twombly. And thanks for helping with everything so I can start the culinary program at the college this fall. The Food Service Technology course I took at the prison was great but I want to get more chef-level cooking training. Plus, the college course covers commercial kitchen management more thoroughly and Dad wants me to run the kitchen at The Coal Bin. I told him I'd love to but he better be prepared to pay for a professional chef." She winked at her father and he winked back.

"You're welcome, Melva. Your family has been a good part of the Twombly business community and the Twombly Foundation is glad to help out. But The Coal Bin's regular customers and the town did more than we did. They did all the fundraisers to help with your dad's medical expenses and volunteered to help at the restaurant and with your dad's physical therapy."

"Yep, that's for sure!" Larry piped up with a big smile on his face. "If it weren't for everyone being so supportive I'd have probably ended up all depressed over my injury. Instead, the town and Georgia, and my Melly Gal kept my spirits up. The whole thing made me see how I'd let everything in my life slide except the business. Now I'm playing wheelchair basketball and got a group of friends that take short walks on the walking path at Okaw Park with our walkers and leg braces. You know. Stuff I'm really enjoying that has nothing to do with work."

"And I love going to the basketball games and cheering them on." Georgia had gotten her husband started in the league.

Larry kissed his wife then reached over and gave his daughter a one-armed hug. "Melva's mom wouldn't have been happy with how I'd gotten, but I think she'd be proud of both of us now. I even talked Melva into trying out for the Twombly College swim team."

"I'm *way* outta shape but I've got some time to get in training and the coaches all know I used to be a strong competitor." Melva leaned into her dad's hug.

There was a lull in the conversation. I was thinking of how it might have gone when Larry found out he'd never walk unaided again, and would be making a lot of use of a wheelchair as well. I was always amazed at the difference positive support from others can make.

"The visitors' center displays about the history and mystery of the Sutton House and Sutton's Lake were very well done," Jebbin said out of nowhere. "Those wonderful shots Nancy took during the dig and Kate's videos bring it to life." His tone changed to something like a cop wheedling a confession from a suspect. "And we have those artifacts that survived the house being buried again. It was sure a good thing that Jairus thought to get the dig team and Ceek together early that Monday evening to get as much of the furnishings and other goods out of the house as were moveable, or there wouldn't be nearly as interesting a display inside the copy of the house."

He looked around at everyone.

"Y'all know, the rugs off the floors, Melvin's desk and Polly's writing table, linens, and lots of other homey objects. Interesting that everything is just credited to Dr. Koerner's dig team, but when

I asked him, he said there were things on display he hadn't seen until they were getting the display cases set up. That someone else had typed up all the information for the files and the display cards before he ever set eyes on them."

I squirmed on the bench beside him. "Ah … um. Yes! Yes, that was … ah, most interesting."

He turned his disapproving professorial glare onto AnnaMay. "And so much of it tied in with period documents, copies of which were generously donated by the Twombly College and Public Library. No denying the pocketwatch found in the house that helped identify Reginald Leander Westford is one of the stars of the display. And the diaries!" Jebbin exclaimed with exaggerated glee. "Those diaries with 'R.L.W.' and 'R.' mentioned in them sure helped, too. And the toys and things from the children's rooms sure make a body glad that the missus and the young'uns had already left."

My face felt hot. We had gone over this more than once during the intervening year.

"Yes. Such wonderful artifacts," I said contritely.

My good man gave me a squeeze. "I'm amazed at the things you end up getting away with."

I was very much the focus of attention, both from the people there who knew all the details and those who hadn't, until now.

And there was still something even Jebbin didn't know. When Melva came home, Madison and I had given her the Sutton girls' two dolls and the dollhouse she had found in the Cornelia House attic.

AnnaMay cleared her throat.

"I think this will be a good time for me to deliver a piece of information that I found during the past year. What you'll be hearing today will not be added to any of the displays or records at the Historical Site."

"Not very nice stuff?" Madison asked.

"Well," AnnaMay shrugged, "perhaps not the most diplomatic to bring up seeing as Peter Westford's older brothers gave a considerable amount of money to help build the replica of the house and purchase the land for the bird sanctuary. They also donated all expenses for the large granite marker north of the roadside over the tunnel, designating the tunnel as the final resting place of both their ancestor, Reginald, and their brother, Peter."

Jairus interrupted. "Everyone on the committee felt it fitting that Reginald's remains be interred under the marker as well, since he had died in the Sutton House in 1844 and the sinkhole the house disappeared into was caused by the tunnel going under the house."

All of us nodded our heads and voiced agreement with the committee's decision.

AnnaMay waited till we were done then continued. "The Westfords know their family comes off badly in all of this, they donated the funds as a sort of restitution, but I don't think we need to make it worse by displaying everything I've found. Peter's brothers decided to leave all the Westford materials that were in our library here at Twombly instead of moving them to Quincy, since it all deals with the time that the family lived in Golden County. So, it's not like it's not there for someone to find some other day."

She looked at us all, gave a firm nod to indicate that was the end of that matter, then continued.

"We know that modern forensics proved that Reginald Leander Westford shot and killed Melvin Sutton. His prints were the only ones on the brass powder flask. It has been assumed that he did so just before the house sank and that he then shot himself when he realized it was that or a slow death while in a house with the corpse of the man he'd murdered. I found proof that assumption was correct. When Emory and I first went through the Westford crates, we'd found a private diary written by Phineas Reginald Westford, Reginald's father."

She paused a moment.

"I'd best explain that some men who were movers and shakers of their time would write diaries they intended to be 'found' after their death that could be published. Diaries of all the good they and their family had done for the community, state, or country. We have several of those written by Phineas. This was not one of those diaries. This was personal and painfully honest. Much of it dealt with Phineas' concerns over Reginald. He knew his son was drinking heavily and was friends with criminals in the area but kept trying to make excuses for him. Even in the May 1844 entries he still seemed to be deluding himself and thinking that Melvin Sutton was leading Reginald astray.

"Last January, I found a page of writing mixed in with other loose papers in one of the wrapped packets of papers that were in the crates. It was written by Phineas Westford, shortly after the July 6th, 1844 flood. Phineas wrote that he had no choice but to believe his son had disappeared along with the house and Melvin Sutton.

"Reginald had left the mansion, he and his wife lived in their own apartment in it, and rode off that night. Phineas was getting tired of not knowing what was happening and followed his son. He went as far as the western crossroad, which was up the slight rise from the house and the flooded farm fields. And he had taken a spyglass with him, hoping that despite the dark and stormy night he'd be able to find out something about what was going on.

"He was able to see that Reginald went into the Sutton's house, *and* more important, he could see through the west-facing window, the one over Polly's writing table, into the master bedroom. He could tell Reginald and Melvin were arguing, he saw his son pull out a pistol and he saw the flash."

We all sat in silent shock. We could hear the sounds of dogs and their owners playing. Children laughing. The smell of our delicious barbeque still hung in the air. A soft summer breeze stirred the leaves of the trees above us.

But I felt chilled to my bones.

"He knew Reginald had shot Melvin." Larry whispered.

AnnaMay sighed. "Yes, and there was more. Phineas wrote that he heard a roar from the northeast, the way Okaw and Rock Creeks flow into the area, just as they do to this day. Then he heard a nearby rumbling and the ground shuddered.

My friend's voice grew softer, sadder.

"According to most accounts, Phineas started losing his mind not long after the flood, and I think I know why. I think he made up the story about Reginald dying on his family's journey to run the business in Quincy to hide what he knew. Not just about his son murdering Melvin Sutton, but that he saw the house with his son in it disappear into the ground and the wall of water that covered it over."

A NOTE TO MY READERS

THE DEVIL'S FLOOD WAS A COMPLICATED AND FASCINATING BOOK TO WRITE, and I hope you have enjoyed it. It is structured a bit differently than the typical cozy mystery, but I wrote it the way it wanted to flow. Some stories just need to go their own ways.

Elements of this story are based on real events and real locations near where I live, but the core of the story—a house that vanishes into a sink hole that is later found and there are mummies in it—is pure fiction. Also as far as I know, although there were several wealthy families in the area at that time, none were like the Twomblys or the Westfords and all the characters, both old and new, are my own creations.

If you would like to learn more about where my ideas for *The Devil's Flood* came from and about the real people and places that helped inspire the story, please go to my website http://www.pearlrmeaker.com and check out the photos and written material there.

Thank you so much for buying and reading my books, and look for the next Emory Crawford Mystery that should be coming out in the fall of 2017.

Hugs,
Pearl

THANK YOU

I COULD NOT WRITE THE EMORY CRAWFORD MYSTERIES WITHOUT THE loving support of my dear husband and our two grown children. I know at times I drive my good man crazy but he tells me to keep on writing. After 40 years he is still the joy of my life!

My editor and writing coach, Mary Rosenblum, is a gem and one of the most patient and tolerant people I've ever known. I truly couldn't do any of this without Mary.

My Uncle John and Aunt Pauline. You two have been so kind. I'm glad to have done you proud—hugs and thanks.

My good friend DC. He and Lyn help me laugh when I need to laugh. He knows what it's like to be a hard working author.

My publisher, Bennett Coles of Promontory Press, and all the wonderful people who work with him. And, my brilliant cover artist, Marla Thompson of Edge of Water Design. It's great to be part of such a wonderful team!

And all of you who read and enjoy the Emory Crawford Mysteries—I write for you. If you have enjoyed your time in Twombly, I've done what I set out to do and I'm a happy camper. ☺

About the Author

Pearl R. Meaker is an upper-middle-aged, short, pudgy homemaker, mother, and grandmother who in 2002 decided to be a writer. She grew up in Dearborn, MI., and has lived most of her life in several states across the American Midwest. She and her husband like small-ish towns more than huge cities. Over the years she's worked different jobs in the various places she has lived, but always came back to being at home with her family. She excels in creative fields, such as writing, music, drama, and art, with hobbies including knitting, crochet, calligraphy, origami, needlepoint, embroidery, counted cross-stitch, very amateur bluegrass fiddling, and both foil and sabre fencing.